AUCTION IN AUSTRALIA

NC ROSS

Trigger and Content Warnings

Explicit language and sex, grief over loss of parent, references to inappropriate touching by a member of a church (no abuse), oblique fat shaming, manipulative parents, discussions of consensual sex work, etc. The main characters work through these issues together.

CHAPTER 1

"Ho-no-ra! Hon-no-ra!" The crowd's chanting carries me offstage as I wave for the last time tonight, my arms falling like jellyfish to my sides. Two encores will exhaust a girl, particularly after six months of nonstop touring.

Adrenaline pumps through my veins, keeping me upright for now, but I know it will leave me cold in a few minutes. It always does.

"Great job tonight!" My friend and backup dancer Billie bumps my hip with hers. "You going to celebrate?"

"In a manner of speaking." I grab my bottle of water, already filled by my invisible team of assistants, and chug half of it. "My parents want to have a chat." What I really need is an açaí bowl and a nap, but no, the universe hands me "an important talk." Where's the fun in being famous if I can never do what I want?

It's better to think of that when I'm not riding an adrenaline high.

Billie groans. "Girl, no. Your parents reminding you yet again of 'everything they've done for you' is not a way to celebrate. You're twenty-three years old and a damned pop superstar. Come out with me."

"Where are you going?" A twinge of jealousy rushes through me. Last time I snuck out with Billie, it did not go well for me.

Her dark brown eyes twinkle. Her short, crimped black hair is still shellacked into a tight ponytail, like all the backup dancers. "Wherever I want. Sydney is full of awesome clubs. You should come. Be young. Get drunk and hook up with some hot rando."

Hah. Like that's even a remote possibility. "You know I can't do that." I twist, hoping to relieve an ache just over the left side of my low back. My sequined costume itches something fierce, and after six months on this tour, there's a smell even my incredible assistants can't get rid of. I can't begrudge them. It's not like this silver and gold fringe minidress with the hand-beaded halter top is easy to dry clean.

Billie huffs. "Look, a purity pledge is fine when you're fifteen and brand-building and your parents are trying to protect you from the predators in this business. But you're not fifteen any more. Live your own life, Nora."

"I want to, it's just that—"

"Honora!"

Both Billie and I wheel around at the intrusion, though we haven't been doing anything wrong. My manager, Marvin Strong, stalks toward us in his dark gray suit, his white hair styled with even more gel than mine. I can't imagine why. It's not like he sweated his ass off for the past two hours onstage. He pauses, casting a cold glance over Billie before settling his gaze on me. "Honora. Excellent job. A little slow on the turns in 'Believe Me,' but I'll have the choreographer work with you first thing tomorrow morning."

A confusing and familiar blend of shame and irritation twist down my spine, tracing the lines of sweat. "Okay, Marvin."

Billie links her arm through mine. "You can't hurt her tonight, Marvin. She killed it out there. All of Sydney wants more Honora."

His phone chimes with what I swear is the world's most generic and awful ringtone. I hear it in my nightmares sometimes. He answers it without even looking up at Billie. "Your parents want to see you immediately. I wouldn't waste their time."

There's a finality in his tone, one I've learned well over the past eight years. I should be grateful, after all. Marvin found one of my videos on social media and hurled me in pop star supernova fame. He made me Honora.

Still, I wish every single day I could just be Nora Grandin again, even if only for five minutes.

I extricate my arm from Billie's, and I feel her deflate beside me. "It's okay. I'll be right there."

CHAPTER 2

I HEAD to my dressing room, smiling and nodding at the university-sized crew of assistants and backup dancers and grips that make my show work. They're busy breaking down the sets, changing into street clothes, or talking about their plans. The excitement is palpable. Tonight was our last night before a two week holiday, one I lobbied hard for and nearly got outvoted on. Which, if I really think about it, makes no sense. Isn't this whole thing about me? Shouldn't I be the one with the final say?

I rarely am. When Marvin, my parents, the record label, and all of the other puppet masters who control my destiny agreed to the holiday, I knew there would be strings attached. I just never quite expect so many.

Which is why, when I push open the door to my dressing room, I'm not surprised to see my parents and my brother

Dawson sitting in the overstuffed armchair and loveseat. They're all Geppettos, only in freshly-pressed Armani.

"Hi, Mom." I bend over and kiss her artificially plumped cheek. She smells like roses and the peppermint gum she chews to hide her smoking from my dad. I don't know why she doesn't realize he'd only notice if a photo showed up on *TMZ*. "Hi, Dad."

He chuffs me on the shoulder like I'm a ball player instead of a pop star. "Hi, Peanut. Great show."

Dawson, perma-smirk in place, glances up from his cell phone before returning to the screen. He and I know full well my dad didn't watch.

"Fixed level 1282 yet?" I ask, sliding onto the stool before my well-lit vanity. My face, a near-perfect replica of my mom's—pre-cosmetic surgery, naturally—is covered with a fine sheen of sweat, but my makeup artist did a great job. The mascara has barely run and my false eyelashes are still in place.

"Working on it," Dawson replies. He designed a video game, a variation of a popular match-three, so he now spends his days checking out the competition in order to make his game better. He's such a lucky jerk. Has he once acknowledged where the money came from so he could have his dream?

But jealousy only gives me a brow furrow that Marvin will want to Botox prematurely, so I tamp it all down, way deep, the way I always do.

I owe them, after all. They're my family. We are meant to love each other, and sometimes love means giving up little pieces of yourself for the good of the whole.

Right?

I stay at the vanity, carefully removing my makeup with the cream-based cleanser and microfiber cloth that don't strip my skin and make me look like I have a communicable disease afterward. Sensitive skin is a blessing and a curse.

"Honora, we need to talk." This can't be good. My dad only uses my legal name if we are in front of the record label or a journalist.

I don't reply. It's easier if I just sit and listen. If I play along, it's only another half hour before I can slip into bed with my books and finally have some peace. If I "make a fuss," it's at least a one hour lecture followed by prayer. I didn't use to mind the praying, but my belief in the church my parents attend has significantly waned over the years. Blame Pastor Curt, that youth leader asshole. I do.

The post-show high has faded, leaving every one of my muscles limp and sore. Dancing in six-inch heels, because I'm considered too short by the record label, does take a toll.

"Wait for it," Dawson grumbles. Uh oh. He rarely has that commiserating tone, which means it's something massive, but I can't fathom what in the world it could be. My parents can't possibly have rethought their decision about not letting me go to college. That's been off the table for years. I can't even let myself ponder getting excited about it. I worked on my speech about why it would be good for me to go to college for months, only to have them shoot me down in less than two sentences.

In contrast, when Dawson asked for money to start his game, they agreed in less than two sentences. Story of my life. I'm the breadwinner, but not the favored child.

"Honey, we found someone for you to marry!" My mom blurts this out, as though it is the single most exciting news in the entire world and she has been holding it in ineffectively.

My hand stills, moisturizing cream covering my fingertips. Am I breathing? I don't think I'm breathing.

They barely let me date. If my mom thought she could

hide an actual chastity belt underneath a silk minidress, I would already have one.

"Honora?" my mother repeats. There is no air in this dressing room. I should call my assistant. The new one, not the one Marvin fired because they were trying to be my friend. Honestly, it's hardly worth learning their names when no one ever lets them— "Honey? Are you all right?"

Static and white noise fill my brain, blocking out everything else. Marriage? Are they out of their minds? This must be Marvin's idea. I can't handle this. I need a very large Black Forest gateau and a coffee drink so full of sugar that it will make my head spin. Not like they let me eat or drink any of those things. My hands clench into fists at my sides, and my nails dig into the skin of my palms. The pain grounds me.

"Honora, answer your mother." My father's voice cuts through the static.

"What the fuck?" My statement lands like an atomic bomb in the middle of the dressing room.

My mom's sharp inhale is the only sound in the room for a long moment. "Don't swear. It isn't polite."

"I'm not sorry." I wheel in my chair to face them. "What the fuck are you talking about? You won't even let me date anyone, and now I'm supposed to get married?"

A flush rises up my mom's neck, but it's my father who replies. "You'll like him. He's a baseball player from somewhere in the Midwest. We'll have a big, lovely wedding. We've already got sponsors lined up."

I croak out a half-sob, half-cackle. "So that makes this okay?" My life flashes before my eyes, and it's surprisingly bleak. A never-ending onslaught of crowds chanting a name I don't want, stadiums and their cavernous backstages, airplane flights when I'm so exhausted I don't even open the window shade or get my free drink. Not that I drink alcohol because Marvin says it makes me too bloated and my costumes won't fit. "I've done everything you've ever asked of me."

"This is the last thing." My mother twirls the gold crucifix at her neck. Her mother gave it to her when I was born. Every time she thinks I'm about to disappoint her, she twists that thing. It's not a crucifix, it's a damned yoke. "I think you're overreacting."

"Overreacting!" My voice echoes in the dressing room, the reverberation shaking the glass jar of chocolate candies I'm not allowed to eat but my parents insist on including in my rider. *Something for you.* Nothing is for me. Not even my body is for me, and how messed up is that? "I'm not overreacting. You're talking about making me marry someone I've never met."

Dawson sits up and sets his phone beside him. I glance toward him. I need my older brother on this. I need an advocate. Just this once. He helped me before, I know he can again. Please.

He shakes his head. It's a small gesture, but I see it. My heart falls even further. Asshole. I should look into how to revoke his monthly allowance, but I only have control over a small portion of my money, and I don't need my parents to know about that little bit of freedom I squirreled away. That's my only ticket out of this mess.

This can't be real. They've done some bananas-level shit over the years—like filming me while I was working on a song at fifteen and sending it to an agent—but I never really thought they would go this far. They're my family.

Shouldn't that count for something?

"Listen." My dad shifts forward, resting his elbows along the knees of the bespoke suit my career bought him. "It's about Jayden."

The word carves a hole in my stomach. So that's the impetus for this.

I don't know why I didn't realize it earlier. Jayden was one of Billie's friends, a choreographer for another show I met when we were in Tokyo. Billie and I snuck out after I pretended to be asleep, and we all met at this sake bar. It was one night. One amazing night. One amazing kiss.

And it all got blown wildly out of proportion, like everything in my life.

The photographer who had been stalking me without my knowledge captured it all on camera, and that's when the shit hit the fan. Hours of hours of commentary on how I didn't really believe in my Purity Pledge. Was Honora really honorable? All of that BS.

No one mentions how unfair it was to Jayden, how the press portrayed him as this sexy sinner when he is really just a nice guy I clicked with once. I tried to apologize to him, and Billie reached out, but he didn't want to hear from me. He shouldn't. I'm massively toxic.

Still. Shouldn't all women have the chance for one nice night? It doesn't mean I need to get married.

"Leave him out of this." I cross my arms across my chest, the spangles chafing against my skin. "I did everything you asked of me after that. I don't go out. I don't see anyone—"

"You still talk to Billie." My father sits upright.

Dread coils deep in my belly. "Don't threaten to fire her again. She's my friend."

"We want you to have friends, honey," my mom interjects. Hah. Yeah, right. "But your dad and I were talking—"

I hold up a hand. "No. You and Dad and *Marvin* were talking."

The flush on her neck deepens to a rich red hue. "It doesn't matter. You know our feelings about waiting until marriage, and you're such a good girl, Nora." Don't think it escapes my notice how now she uses the name I actually prefer. "But you're twenty-three. You're a woman now."

Ah, yes. Maybe she's referring to the extra-creepy tabloid spreads and online memes that pay particular attention to the growth of my breasts and ass. Nothing like being sexualized on the worldwide web and enduring the myriad glances of bottom-dwellers to turn you off the very idea of sex.

"If I'm a woman, that means I get to make my own choices." There's an edge of steel to my voice that I like. It clears the rest of the static from my brain. These people don't care about me, not really. I've lived my whole life trying to get them to love me, and all they love is what I can do for them. Fuck that. "I'm not letting someone else decide who I'm going to marry or who I'm going to have sex with."

My mother inhales again sharply when I say the word 'sex.' I can't imagine why, when that's exactly what she's talking about.

"Don't think I don't know what's going on." I stand and loom over my parents on the loveseat. Six-inch heels may be a curse on stage, but they're quite effective in this smaller space. "Marvin wants to sell my virginity to some highest bidder in what I imagine is going to be a very well publicized and highly photographed event, all of which will then be further merchandized. Thus making you and Marvin, less so me, shitloads of cash. None of this bothers you and your Church of Righteous Indignation, Mom?"

She closes her eyes tightly, and a small sliver of regret at my words cuts through me. I've never insulted her religious beliefs before. I know how much they mean to her, how much they used to mean to me. But that was before they turned me into a commodity. I'm not the eight-year-old in a white lace pinafore with my hair in ringlet curls any longer. "This is fucking ridiculous," I say. Tears well up and I run behind the changing screen to get out of this awful, itchy, smelly, sweaty costume.

"Honora." My dad's voice slices through the thin fabric of

the changing screen. "We need to discuss this. Your fiancé is flying into Sydney tomorrow. You'll meet. If he's not heinous, we are going to proceed with this. We won't have you involved in some sex scandal."

How do neither of them realize that selling me off to some random baseball player because I have to maintain this stupid chastity image is *also* a sex scandal? I grab my black hoodie and pull on my dark gray knitted leggings and hot pink sneakers.

"Dad," Dawson interjects. "Maybe we should—"

"Stay out of this, son."

I step out from behind the changing screen and pull my gross, concert-sweaty blonde hair into a messy bun on top of my head. "Yeah, Dawson. Don't stand up for me or anything."

He grimaces. "Nora, you know I want to help you."

"Not as much as you want to help yourself." I grab my bag, which only has a book, my sunglasses, a photo ID, and my phone. I don't know where I'm going, but I won't need much. For fuck's sake, they won't even let me carry my own hotel room key.

"Honora. Don't you dare leave this room!" My dad's face is a purplish mass of rage. I've never walked out before. I've never said no like this before.

It's past time.

"Fuck all of you," I say, and I slam the door so hard I feel the echo of the rattle deep in my bones.

CHAPTER 3

uke

"ALL IN." I push my chips across the green felt of the card table. It's a fucking miracle I don't knock them all to the ground, since my heart is racing so fast and my hands barely feel like they're a part of me. But I'm not shaking. I'm not sweating. No.

It's all my money, everything I've managed to save over the years. It was meant to set up a new business, whenever I decide what the fuck I want to do with my life. It's everything my dad told me to do: save up, make a life for yourself. If I lose...but I won't. I can't. I have four sevens. There's no way Tobias can beat that.

Then I'll be sailing clear. No more worries, no more angry messages on my mom's voicemail from asshole debt collectors. I can pay off her house and upgrade her insurance to one that will actually pay for the immune therapy she needs. I'll finally fulfill every promise I ever made to my dad's memory.

Maybe I'll have a little leftover, too, for that as-yet-unknown dream.

Tobias chews the wad of his unlit cigar, his expression stoic. If I didn't hate him because I need his money and his game, I'd admit that he's not a bad looking guy, a George Lazenby type in a brown tweed overcoat with professor patches on the elbows. "You sure you can handle that, Bautista?" His Australian accent is thick, but I've lived in Sydney long enough to parse it by now. "Wouldn't want the likes of you getting stuck in my country."

Great. He knows I live here and have for the past two years. Still, it's always fun to see the judgment toward my chosen profession in action. Whatever. It will be that much sweeter when I beat him and take the hundred thousand in chips lying on the table.

Think of Mom. Mom and Dad, dancing together in the living room of our house in Wisconsin. Mom in the same living room after Dad's funeral, staring mutely at a spot of people wallpaper he never had time to fix. I won't think about me, about how I lost almost everyone I loved in the span of two bleak months.

There's a good reason I've chosen the job I have, and it's because true love is fleeting.

"Let's do this," I say. I doubt he can hear the pounding of my heart in my chest. I've worked hard on my poker face, hewn from years of watching and working in BDSM clubs. Four of a kind is a great hand, one of the best. There's no way he can win. "I'll even sweeten the pot. An extra hundred."

"You don't have that kind of cash." He narrows his dark gray eyes. Behind him, his enforcers glare at me.

"I wouldn't wager if I didn't have it." My voice sounds

surprisingly even. It was tough even coming up with the fifty grand I've already laid out on the table. Student loans, funeral costs, and medical expenses eat into every single paycheck I have. If I win—no, when I win—I'll finally have a buffer. Maybe I can take some time off from Leather and Lace, from other people's fantasies, and figure out once and for all what I want to do with my life. I need this. I deserve this. God can't hate me that much. "What's wrong, Tobias? Cash flow problems?"

I probably shouldn't poke the bear, but it's taken me months to get into this game. Months of working connections from L and L, months of listening to my mom's exhausted voice over myriad phone calls. *"No, honey, don't worry, I'll figure something out,"* she says. Every. Single. Time. But there's nothing to figure out. She hasn't worked in months, not since her diagnosis and the traditional chemo left her too weak to do much of anything but live on my dad's paltry social security and what I can spare. This is my responsibility. I'm all she has now, and if it means I need to poke the bear, then so fucking be it.

"You're a right bogan." Tobias's mouth twists around the stub of cigar in his mouth. "It's your funeral." He gestures to one of the Central Casting dropouts behind him, who takes out a piece of paper and hands it to Tobias. He scrawls his name and the amount before dropping it into the ante pile.

My heart pounds, but I've got this. That's a shit ton of money on the table. But the universe owes me. Haven't I been good? Or, not exactly *good*, but I've helped people. I treat others with respect. Consent is king. *Give me this one win, please.* I'm way past overdue.

I lay out my cards on the table— spade, diamond, club, and heart. "Four of a kind." My voice is triumphant, my posture straight. Maybe my dad wouldn't love the gambling aspect, but his unexpected death and its aftermath meant I had to make choices. Won't he be proud I'm doing what it takes to care for Mom?

Tobias doesn't grin or make any other motion other than to toss his cards face up on the table. It's a casual gesture, one of defeat, surely. My spirit soars. This is it. Finally. My one win.

But then I get a look at his cards.

Shit.

"Straight flush, Bautista. Bad luck."

Double shit.

My muscles react before my brain catches up, and I sprint for the door. The hulking goons are faster, though, and a fist slams hard into my left kidney. Pain explodes across my back and down my spine, momentarily blinding me and stealing all my air. I groan and slump to the floor.

I see Tobias's thick brown boots stop before me, but I can't get up from the spasms wreaking havoc in my back. He clucks his tongue like a disapproving nun. "I take it you don't have my money." He drops to his knees before and takes a knife out of his belt. Behind me, Goon One yanks back on my thick black hair, pulling my head up. Running the blade between his fingers, Tobias makes sure I see everything.

"Not the face. Please." I hate the whiny edge to my voice, but I can't do anything about it now. "Without my face, I can't work. I can't get your money."

My dad never would have done this. He never would have gotten involved with fucking mobsters to get the money. He never would have lost.

He must be so disappointed in me.

Tobias runs the point of the blade over my thick black eyebrows. "Even your mug can't earn you a hundred grand in a week, Pretty Boy."

Aww, he cares.

"I'll get your money, Tobias." I have no idea how. He's

right, which burns like acid in my stomach. It took me two years to save the fifty grand I brought to this table. But I have to come up with something. I can't leave my mom alone.

"Yes, you will." He runs the blunt edge of the knife across my cheek, and I try not to squirm. He cuts me and I might as well throw myself to the sharks off Bondi Beach. "You have one week. If you don't have my money by then, your face will be the last of your worries."

How the fuck am I going to come up with a hundred thousand dollars in one week?

ora

Where the hell am I?

I managed to sneak out of the stadium because everyone's too busy closing down the tour for the next two weeks to notice me. Still. I've been to Sydney before, but only in a car from the hotel to the venue then straight back. It's not like I know where I'm going.

I'm out in the front of the stadium in Olympic Park, which faces a tree-lined pedestrian only zone, lit at this time of night by streetlights and the gleam of a few bars that are open to capture the people exiting the concert. It's too dark to see much else, and I doubt I can figure out the subway system in my current state of mind.

The glow of cell phone screens is ubiquitous, the blue light nauseating me.

There are far too many people here, all of whom have recently seen me shaking my ass and singing until my lungs ache on stage. Call me paranoid, but I think it's understand-able given my history. Everyone has a camera.

I can't hide here.

Wending my way out the back through the departing crowds, I scan the taxi and ride share queues, but both of them are way too unruly for me to hide. I wish I had a mask of some kind, but all I have is the hood of my sweatshirt, which I wrap around my face and pull the drawstring.

Billie. I can call Billie. I head for a discreet corner and text her as I'm walking. She gets back to me almost immediately with a meme of a toddler jumping up and down and screaming "hell yeah."

A hint of relief settles in my shoulders. Salvation is on the way.

"So what happened this time?" Billie asks from the driver's seat of her rental car. I haven't spoken in the twenty minutes it took us to get out of the post-concert traffic, but I finally crawled out of the well beneath the seat so I can actually look out the window.

It's dark but the freeway is well-lit, and the city beyond looks like so many other places I've been. I may be an international traveler, but so much of my experience is this peri-highway view, full of concrete noise-blocking walls, red lights, and exit ramps.

I wind my hands into the cuffs of my hoodie. It's not like Billie doesn't know my family. The whole myth of Honora is very tightly wound with my infamous Purity Pledge. I've minded a few times over the years, but I've always been too busy and exhausted even to think about sex, so I never protested it before. And it protected me for a long time from men who only wanted to take. Still, I didn't really think my family would do something like this. Why does it hurt so much? "I'm in luck. My parents have found a man to marry me."

The brakes squeal as Billie pulls over to the side of the road and stops the car, her brown eyes wide as caverns. "What. The. Fuck."

It makes me feel a little less like I'm living in Bizarro-World. "See? This is an appropriate response."

Billie still stares at me, her mouth hanging so far open I wonder if I should close it.

"Are you broken, Billie?" The joke feels hollow as I say it. The tears that had receded when she came to pick me up now threaten to overwhelm me. I can't believe they're doing this. Actually, I can, and that's worse.

I thought I would have one thing that would be my decision, one thing that would be my choice, and they're taking that from me like they've taken everything else. What am I but a hollow shell in a pretty dress with a vicious fear of vocal cord nodes?

Snapping to attention, Billie shakes her head, her cropped, pixie-cut black hair barely moving. She wipes away the tears under my eyes with a quick swish of her thumb. "I can't believe your parents would do something this messed up. Tell me what happened."

I pull my sweatshirt more tightly around my body. "It's like *Game of Thrones,* or something. Not that I've ever had time even to watch that show the whole way through."

"Skip the last season. Not worth it." Billie settles into her seat, her face open, ready to listen. Thank God for Billie. If I didn't have her…

I don't want to think about that.

"They think that since I'm now twenty-three, I'm incapable of making my own decisions regarding my body. My virginity is under threat and I'll just throw it away on a stranger. Like I do reckless things all the time." I choke on a sob halfway through my statement. "So they're arranging some publicity stunt marriage. It's—it's—"

Billie digs through her crossbody bag and finds a tissue, which she hands to me. "Completely fucking ridiculous."

I try to laugh but it devolves into a massive sob, one that has me shaking and bent over. Billie rubs my back in slow circles, and her presence is helpful, but it's also making me feel incredibly guilty. She's young, too. She doesn't need all my personal drama. Still, she is the only one who is here, the only one I can talk to. I had thought Dawson…but no. Even my brother wouldn't come to my rescue.

It's just like how I feel when I'm performing in a stadium, alone in a massive crowd of humanity.

"It's all so stupid," I say as my sobs let up. "I hate that word, but that's how it feels. I'm rarely—if ever—alone with anyone. I'm so exhausted after practicing and exercising and smiling like a damned doll I've barely considered having sex. But I always thought it would be my choice. That I would be able to convince them that it's ridiculous and backward and patriarchal to continue the Purity Pledge shit. I just wanted it to be my choice." As it rolls off my tongue, the curse word makes me feel powerful.

Billie keeps rubbing my back, her expression pensive. "Maybe you need to show them."

"How?"

There's a bright gleam in her eyes, one that looks like she's about to tell me we need to ditch class and go smoke behind the bleachers. I'm frustrated and angry enough to do anything.

"Maybe it's time to lose your V card on your own terms."

CHAPTER 5

ora

THIS IS A TERRIBLE IDEA. Terrible, but wonderful, too. Billie is right. If this entire arranged marriage thing is designed to force me to lose my virginity in a creepy parent-approved way, then I'll do it on my own terms. It will be *my* choice.

Since I don't have any boyfriends ready to jump in, why not find a professional?

Which is why I stand beside Billie at the check-in desk for a club called Leather and Lace. She didn't have any extra clothes in her car, so I'm still in my hoodie and leggings, but the incredibly sexy woman with golden brown skin, long dark curls, and a fire-engine red bustier doesn't seem to care. Her smile is warm as she hands me back my ID.

"Welcome to Leather and Lace. Would you like me to call someone to give you a tour?"

"No, thanks." Billie links her arm with mine, and it's

enough to make me stop ogling the woman. "I've been to one of your other locations."

"Wonderful!" The woman's smile stretches across her entire face, like maybe she is a preschool teacher in her day job. "You two are in luck. It's Auction Night." She reaches behind the desk and hands both of us black, lacy masks. "You'll need these."

"Thank you. This is going to be awesome." Billie's tone betrays her excitement as she takes the masks.

The woman rises, and below the bustier she is wearing skin-tight red leather pants. She pulls back the curtain. "Have fun. If you need any help, just ask. Feel free to look around. Everyone here gets vetted. Safety first."

That's good to know. I tie Billie's mask in place and she does the same for me, and then we link arms and enter the club. I'm grateful for the mask. It gives me power. No one here will know I am Honora Grand. I can be anyone, anything.

Though when we walk in, I'm thrilled Billie is beside me.

I mean, I'm not a complete noob. I've been to dance clubs several times, often to meet with other musicians or producers or whatnot.

This is not that kind of club.

"So, you've been here before?" I ask Billie. As we enter, two women, both wearing the bare minimum, slow dance in front of us. One of them pulls aside the collar of the other woman's shirt and traces kisses along her collarbone. My libido has been in perma-exile, but even I have to admit, it's hot. The way they move together, the way they seem so oblivious even to the crowd around them. What would that be like, to have someone so into me? To have that power over them and in myself?

Maybe this wasn't *such* a terrible idea.

"I've been to their club in New York. It's amazing. It's

kink-friendly, and everyone is super nice, even if you just want to sit and have a drink." Billie points to the bar and I follow her. This room is huge and set up a little like a dinner theater. Tables and stuffed banquettes and chairs are sprinkled across the floor with a large stage at the front. Hallways with buff men in suits guarding them spread out from the floor. Across the room, an older man in full leather straps and a ball gag sits patiently beside a younger blonde woman sipping a martini. Onstage, there is a woman with smooth brown skin and a cascade of rich dark and golden brown curls. She is dressed in a sleek teal sheath dress and holds a tablet in one hand while adjusting a microphone with another.

We slide into two open seats at the bar, and I nod toward the woman. "Is that for the auction?"

"Yes." The bartender appears before us, a warm smile on his tanned face and his Australian accent thick and delicious. "That's Asta, one of the heads of the company. She's here for a few weeks. Can I get you anything to drink?" He's wearing a black vest and dark jeans and looks like all the best kinds of sin. So far, he's the only one I've seen here in the club without a mask.

My mouth goes a little dry, even as my heartbeat races. *I can't do this.* I can't just randomly pick some guy up at a bar. I've never done that even when I wasn't looking to pop my cherry. How do I know I can trust them? How do I know—

Billie elbows me in the side, interrupting my own personal spiral. "Get a drink, Nora. It will make you feel better."

"We have a two drink limit," the bartender says, but his voice is soft and helpful. "Consent is held above all else here, and even if your inhibitions are lower, you still need to be able to understand whatever it is you're looking for."

Billie orders a Hendrick's and soda, and I blindly order

one, too. I don't drink much. Hell, there are a lot of things I don't do and it's time to change that.

"Are you okay?" Billie asks.

"I think so." I glance around the room. I'm very under-dressed but no one seems to care. I could be wearing nothing and fit right in. People seem very…free. At one table, two men kiss each other like it is all they want to do and the kiss itself is the destination. It's gorgeous and sexy and it's doing something to my body that makes me tingle all over. "Everyone's already paired up, though."

"Not everyone." The bartender re-appears with two tall glasses garnished with lime wedges. "Don't worry. You two will have no trouble attracting attention, depending on what you're into. And then there's always the auction."

Billie leans forward on her stool, resting her elbows on the bar. "Tell us about the auction. I've never seen one."

The bartender grins. "We run different ones, but tonight it's a bachelor auction. People volunteer their time, the professionals and some regulars as well. It's a one week commitment, all kinks and requests ironed out at the time of the auction. It's a lot of fun."

"People have the time to take a week off to have sex with each other?" Okay, I realize as I'm saying that how naïve I sound, but the bartender merely shrugs.

"There are worse ways to spend a week, love. Enjoy your drinks." With that, he moves off down the bar.

Onstage, an extremely good-looking man with thick black hair and a solid black mask covering the top half of his face interrupts Asta, who has finished setting up the micro-phone and now taps frantically on her tablet. Something low in my stomach curls and warms me. Even if I can't see his face, his body in his fitted flight attendant uniform is a thing of a beauty. He looks kind, too, if a little stressed. He winces as he turns toward Asta, like his back hurts.

Relatable. As if in sympathy, my own back twitches, and I stretch discreetly.

"This place is awesome, isn't it?" Billie sips her drink and makes a happy, pleased squeal. "Do you see anyone you might want to talk to?"

I glance around, my gaze catching on the flight attendant before I move on, but it's all a little too overwhelming. My heart won't stop racing. "I think maybe this is a terrible idea."

"Not terrible at all," a deep voice beside me says. "If it takes this for us to meet, maybe this is a good thing."

uke

"Please, Asta. Let me into the auction." I stand beside my boss, helping her as she sets up the stage. I bend over to move the microphone cord out of the way, and a spasm seizes the area around my left kidney. I inhale sharply, swallowing the pain. Asta's a hell of a boss, but she doesn't need to know I'm not at one hundred percent.

The click of her heels echoes, even in the crowded room. "Don't you have enough to do already? You only just got home, what? Six hours ago? You need a rest."

Okay, so yes, I went straight from my last flight—direct Singapore to Sydney, acting as a fourth for the trio's poly play—and didn't even stop at my minuscule apartment before I got fleeced by Tobias. Desperate times, desperate measures. "I can rest on a seven day paid vacation with a lucky winner." I wink, and earn myself a well-deserved eye roll. "Please. I need this. And so do you. I'm sure you don't have enough bachelors."

She frowns with one corner of her mouth, convincing me that I'm right, so I push it. I have to. I've done these auctions before and it's a great way to earn some quick cash, even if it won't be the full hundred grand. Even twenty thousand might buy me a few days, maybe even another week. Then, if Tobias and his asshole friends are really going to shake me down—which I doubt not even a little bit—I can use the rest to disappear and disappear fast.

"Besides." I gesture toward where her boyfriend Alaric sits at a table, staring up at her with his silver leather collar discreetly tucked behind his tie. "Alaric can't do it. He would do anything for you, but I know you're not into cuckolding."

She grimaces and sighs. Triumph soars in my chest. I was hoping she would cave. "Fine. But next time use the damned Sign Up Genius form like everyone else, and *on time* please." She taps on her screen with the stylus, adding my name to the roster. "I see Danica gave you a mask. Are you going to change?"

I glance down at my Leather and Lace Travel uniform. I didn't have a ton of time to change before I warped my life into a hell dimension at a poker game. "It's clean. Mostly. I'll undo the top few buttons. People will love it."

She rolls her large brown eyes, then taps on the headset speaker over her ear. "Harrison?" That's the bartender. A very good man, and a very good Dom when he wants to be. "What do you mean? Oh."

I follow her concerned gaze toward the bar, where a graying white man in a full-on devil's mask is hitting on two very pretty young women. Neither of them are interested, their body language very pointedly against the guy, but he can't take a hint. Harrison stands at the opposite end of the bar, glancing between the women and Asta on stage. He's mixing drinks but unable to help.

"Sergei?" Asta says into her headset, but whatever reply she gets isn't what she's hoping for.

"I'll get it." I wave a farewell to Asta and immediately head down to the bar. Gray Devil leans way too close to the blonde woman in the black hoodie.

I squeeze between Gray Devil and the blonde, who smells a little like sweat but also a lot like the beach when it rains, like pure sunshine. No wonder Gray Devil sought her out.

"Hey, babe. Sorry I'm late." I use a light Aussie accent, because might as well blend in with the locals. Gotta love high school drama club.

I'd slide my arm around her but her friend gives me an expression between bemusement and if-you-touch-her-they'll-never-find-your-body, so I content myself with leaning on the bar and staring down Gray Devil. "Nice mask. Tell me, have you ever heard the word 'subtle?'"

I imagine he frowns at me, but it's impossible to tell behind his ridiculous mask. "You're together?" He nods at both women.

"Absolutely." The blonde woman's friend, the one with the pixie cut who is dressed appropriately for the club in a low-cut black bodycon dress, kisses her friend's cheek. "We're good with three."

To my astonishment, the cute blonde woman blushes, the redness flowing up her neck. Maybe this is her first time. I always like a newbie.

"Fine," Gray Devil grumbles. He picks up his glass of what smells like Scotch and heads to find easier prey.

I back up, giving the women space, but I'm not ready to leave yet. Blondie looks young, but there's a fierceness in those green eyes of hers that draws me in.

"Thanks for that." Pixie Cut sips her drink and squeezes her friend's shoulder. "I didn't think that guy would leave."

"No problem." I shrug. "I've been a lot of people's pretend boyfriend. It's not often I'm part of a pretend threesome."

"Oh my God." Blondie turns away from me and drinks half her cocktail.

"Was it something I said?" I lean closer, enjoying the way the heat rises up her neck. "If this is your first time here, definitely don't go looking for the throne room."

Blondie shakes her head, like she refuses to listen to me. It's cute and very appealing.

"Let's start again," I say. I hold out my hand, and Pixie Cut takes it. "I'm Ludo." Sometimes, but I'm here in my professional capacity so I'm not about to give them my real name.

"Billie. This is Nora." Her gaze cuts to Blondie's for a moment, then flicks back to me. Interesting. "Do you work here?"

"Sometimes."

Nora doesn't look up from her cocktail. "You're wearing a flight attendant uniform."

"I know. Hot, right?" I unclasp the top three buttons, exposing a few inches of chest. I work hard for it, so I might as well show it off.

"Do you just wear the uniform?" Nora asks.

"No, I am also a flight attendant." I slide onto the bar stool beside her. "I just flew in from Singapore."

"And boy are your arms tired." She drains the rest of her drink.

I laugh, mostly at her extra dry delivery. "Do you want another?" I point at her glass.

"No." She shakes her head emphatically. I wonder what she looks like behind that lacy black mask. It doesn't matter. I like her anyway. "Maybe a club soda. I'm not a big drinker."

"Me neither." I signal Harrison and he comes over to take our orders. "Two club sodas with lime." He nods approvingly. He should be pleased I chased Gray Devil away.

"I'm going to find the ladies' room," Billie says, her dark brown eyes twinkling. I cast her a grateful nod.

"No, wait—" but Billie doesn't listen to Nora before she's gone.

"So." I sip my club soda, the cold bubbles licking down my throat. "Have you ever been in a club like this?"

"No." She has her hands scrunched up in the cuffs of her hoodie, which is incredibly endearing. "It's...different. Everyone is just so out there."

"Better than being closeted. Leather and Lace isn't that kind of place."

"Really?" She tilts her head. "Is it from outer space and off its face?"

The laugh this time catches me even more by surprise. "You're not having a great night, huh?"

"Nope." She plays with the straw in her glass, but her posture has softened a bit since Gray Devil has gone. "Definitely not."

"What brings you here?"

At this, she sighs and turns toward me. The lace of the mask cups her cheeks, and there's a depth of sorrow in those green eyes that cuts through me. "I don't know. I—I freaked out, and Billie rescued me. Maybe this isn't the right thing for me."

"Hmm." I tilt toward her. Whatever it is she has been doing earlier tonight, she smells clean and fragrant. "What are you looking for? A place like this, we cater to all your fantasies."

"Even flight attendant ones?" Her lip quirks upward in one corner, but her gaze catches on the small swath of skin I exposed.

"Leather and Lace Travel is special." I watch as she sips her club soda, her lips wrapping around the straw. It can rapidly become my new kink. "It's a kink-focused travel agency. We want people to experience whatever they desire."

"Meaning sex?" she asks. Her voice is soft, but firm, like she's making a decision.

"Sometimes." I tilt my head to the side, still watching her. "Most of the time."

Her breath audibly catches in her throat. "Sex with you?"

Smiling, I don't hesitate. I'm not ashamed of what I do. There's a lot to like about my job. Keeping it professional means no one ever stomps all over my heart before tossing the ragged edges into the trash. Even if I'm attracted to this mystery Nora, I can maintain my emotional distance. Things I've lived and learned. "Sometimes. Most of the time."

My answer doesn't seem to startle her, nor does she look at me like she's ready to jump me, which is refreshing. "I play a lot of roles in my life," I say. "I can be a lot of things to a lot of people, and I like it that way." It's vastly preferable to dealing with my own shit. Being someone else means I never have to face the hurt I buried years ago.

She meets my gaze, but she plays with the straw in her glass. "Who are when you're not playing a role?"

There's curiosity tinged with heat in her tone, and it calls to me. I lean forward, my nose inches from hers. She inhales sharply, just once, but her gaze is determined.

"Who are you, Nora?" I ask.

There's a moment—no, an instant really—where her green eyes flare with desire. Like she's wondering how I taste.

Relatable. I'm wondering exactly the same thing.

Before she can answer, before I can close the last few inches and kiss those luscious lips, Asta's voice echoes through the room.

"Hello, Sydney! Let's get started with our Bachelor Auction."

ora

"Him." Billie points at Ludo on stage, where he has now fully unbuttoned his uniform shirt, displaying a very excellent set of golden brown muscles.

"What?" I'm still having trouble breathing. Something about the way he talked to me was so intimate, even though we were just chatting. It was like he could see past the mask and into my very soul. "No."

"No?" Billie's eyes widen. She just returned from the bathroom, which I suspect was a horrible ruse to leave me alone with the World's Sexiest Man. "He's perfect."

"I don't know. I'm rethinking the whole thing."

"No." Billie takes my hands and forces me to look into her eyes. "What will you do then, Nora? Huh? Are you going to go back to your hotel and marry some fucking stranger like a good little eighteenth century princess? No. The main benefit of waiting to have sex is you don't need to mess around with the initial teenage groping and premature ejaculation. You could have sex with *him.*"

She points again toward Ludo. In my career, I have met many fabulously good-looking people. It happens at parties and events all the time. Still, none of them quite hold a candle to Ludo with his thick black hair and dark brown eyes. A girl could lose herself in those eyes.

I almost did.

Onstage, he catches me looking at him and casts me a smile. My stomach swoons. Talk about being an eighteenth century princess.

"He's a sex worker." I keep my voice low, because now people are congregating around us at the bar. Everyone wants to watch the auction, I suppose.

"So what? He's a nice guy who saved you with the fake boyfriend thing, and a professional means your first time will be good." Billie rolls her eyes back in her head and bites her lip. "Like, soooo good."

"Why don't you do it?"

Billie shrugs. "I don't have your money. I haven't been to one of these before, but I'm guessing these men aren't going for pocket change."

She can't be wrong. There are six of them onstage, including Ludo, and every single masked one looks like he has been ordered from a catalog of Perfect Male Specimens.

The bidding starts on the first one in the lineup, a tall, blond man who looks like a cross between a young Arnold Schwarzenegger and a surfer. "The bidding starts at five thousand," the announcer says.

I finish my club soda. "We should go. I'm tired."

Billie squeezes my hand. "Nora, you're exhausted. But you're exhausted because your manager runs you ragged and you haven't had a proper vacation for as long as I've known you. Even when you're not touring or performing, you're giving interviews, or recording, or exercising. It's always something. You never take a break. You *deserve* this. It's seven days with one gorgeous man. Even if you don't have sex with him, maybe you can chill out and reset."

Okay, that does sound appealing, and she has a point. My parents have always pushed me to keep moving. A person's staying power in the industry is about as secure as quicksand. But perpetual motion leads to permanent exhaustion and a twinge in my lower back that never quite goes away. Not to mention the emotional whirlpool of constantly wishing they would look at me as *me* and not as their meal ticket.

That will never happen as long as I keep following their rules.

The first bachelor sells for thirty thousand to a male-male couple, and they all look thrilled at the prospect. A kernel of heat twirls deep in my belly. People are going to have sex tonight. They're probably already having sex somewhere in this club. For the first time, maybe I can, too. My family isn't here to intervene or chaperone. I'm free.

"Where does the money go?" I ask.

"Most goes to the bachelor," the bartender announces, sliding a fresh club soda and lime my way. "Asta keeps twenty percent and donates it to a local charity. Here, it's a wildfire relief fund."

That's reassuring. The man doing the work gets to keep the profit. I think of my secret offshore account, the one I set up four years ago when I realized my parents weren't going to budge about me attending college. I filled it by siphoning bits over the last few years, whenever I thought Marvin wouldn't notice. There's over four million in it now, a miniscule fraction of my net worth, but at least it's all mine. My rainy day fund, because I think I always knew that they would pull something like this, and

I'd need to flee. A girl needs money of her own in this world.

Ludo walks up to the announcer and combs a hand through his sheaf of dark hair. Desire twists up my spine and I shift on my barstool. A girl needs money of her own and control over her own body.

Billie follows my gaze. "Rest is resistance, Nora. And that man? For even an hour with him, I'd be a freedom fighter."

"We have a special last-minute addition to our lineup tonight," Asta says beside Ludo. "One of our long-time employees at Leather and Lace, Ludo. What does Ludo specialize in, besides making sure your tray table is in its upright and locked position?" Here Ludo flexes his bicep, and several people in the audience applaud. "He's a master of romance, a switch who likes it every which way, whatever your pleasure is. And if you win a week with Ludo, make sure to ask for his signature massage."

"Ten thousand!" An overly tanned man at one of the tables calls out.

"Fifteen!" A Black woman wearing a leather catsuit holds up a whip.

Billie elbows me in the side. I've never attended an auction of anything before, and it moves too rapidly for me to keep up. I can hear the rising numbers, though. Thirty thousand. Fifty. Seventy-five.

"Two hundred thousand." This from the Gray Devil, the creepo who hit on me. Ludo's casual smirk tightens, and his gaze flicks to me, then to the announcer. It's a blink of connection, but I feel it in every nerve of my body. Gray Devil shouldn't get the week with Ludo. I should. I should have attention on my own terms.

"Two fifty." When I speak, it feels like all eyes latch onto me, but I could care less. I stand, and even in my leggings and messy bun, I feel powerful. We are made of our choices in this world, and I'm fucking sick of having all mine taken from me.

I choose this. I choose him.

"Three hundred." Gray Devil narrows his gaze at me. He knows full well Ludo isn't my boyfriend, and he doesn't like the interference. Well, screw him. I've dealt with way too much fragile masculinity today, and Billie is right. I deserve this. I deserve a week away from my overbearing manager and my non-supportive family.

"Five hundred thousand."

All noise in the club abruptly comes to a halt. Billie's excitement is an explosion of silent energy beside me. I glance at Gray Devil, but it's impossible to see his expression behind that ridiculous mask. Onstage, Ludo wears a look of shock that he quickly hides. He turns to Asta and whispers something in her ear.

"Sold!" Asta says. "To the generous young woman at the bar. You'd better treat her right, Ludo."

CHAPTER 8

uke

I DON'T MISS Asta's very perceptive glare as I head down the stairs to the bar where this week's girlfriend sits. Thank goodness. Gray Devil looks a little too sadistic for me. I don't mind bondage or a little pain, but he would get off on pushing me to the very edge of my limits.

Nora won't. Now that I can see her, sitting there at the bar, talking in hushed, anxious tones with her friend, she looks like she is reconsidering this whole thing.

She can't reconsider. Half a million dollars. Even with the twenty percent for the club donation, that's enough money to pay off my debt to Tobias, Mom's medical bills, and hire a private caregiver until she gets back on her feet. This is way more than I even could have potentially dreamed of earning from the auction. Whatever else, Nora can't back out now.

Time for Charm.

"You saved my bacon." I slide onto the bar stool beside

her, and Billie steps back to give us space. "I thought I was going to have the spend the week in the dungeon getting edged by Gray Devil."

Billie snorts into her drink, but Nora pales.

Harrison appears before me with two tall glasses of club soda and lime. "Want a bit of vodka in it?" he asks Nora.

"Yes," she replies quickly, not looking up from the floor.

Billie holds out her hand toward me. "I need your ID."

"My ID?" My hand reaches for my wallet even before she answers. I am a people pleaser, after all.

"You could be a serial killer. This is insurance, to make sure Nora will be ok."

"That totally makes sense." It's an Australian driver's license and uses my stage name, so I'm not too worried. I doubt Billie has any connection to my family in Wisconsin.

I watch as Billie takes a photo of my ID with her phone and then hands it back to me.

Nora looks green, and I doubt it's because the blonde hair isn't real. When Harrison delivers her vodka soda, she drinks nearly half of it.

"You don't have to be nervous." I lean against the bar. "I'm yours, darl. Whatever you want. One week." Usually the Australian accent is a panty dropper. Maybe I should have gone with the Spanish. Being half Filipino helps when you live your life in near-constant role play. Nobody can place me, and I like it that way.

Nora doesn't reply, and Billie elbows her. This is going to be a challenge. What's her hang up? Please tell me she has the money. I really don't want to be thrown back into the fray. Gray Devil keeps glancing over at us like he's interested in a ménage.

I can't let her back out. Five hundred thousand, in one week. It's a dream come true.

Time to do my thing. I take Nora's hand in mine. Her skin

is soft and warm and her fingers are slightly callused, like she spends a lot of time holding a pen but not doing hard labor. I trace between the bones of her hand with my thumb until she raises her gaze to mine. There's fight in her, a determination I respect that is supernova-level hot. Still, I don't want to overwhelm her. "Look. I know this is all a lot. It's a late night, this is a new club and a new situation. We have time. Why don't you go back to your hotel and —"

"No." Nora sits upright, her spine almost completely straight. "No, I don't want to go there."

Interesting. My brow wrinkles, but that's just going to give me a migraine. "Okay. We don't have to go there."

Nora glances at Billie, but she shrugs. "They'll come looking for you in my room," Billie says, almost too softly. Lucky for me I have supernatural hearing abilities. Okay, not really. Who are these people and why can't we go to their hotel room?

It's not my place to question. It's my job to perform and get paid. I'm not going to get embroiled in…whatever this is. This type of intrigue has never helped me in the past.

Asta approaches us, her strides assured. "Hello." She holds out a hand to Nora, who shakes it. "I have here the contract for you and Ludo. Any questions?"

"No." Nora's swallow practically echoes in the room. "Where do I pay?"

"Here." Asta holds out a bank transfer form, and Nora fills it out promptly. Wow, a girl who knows her routing number. Kinky. "Are you sure there's nothing you need? Ludo will take very good care of you." Her gaze cuts into me like she will be watching. Trust me, I know. Asta's many things, but she always insists on enthusiastic consent, and I wholeheartedly agree.

"Um." Billie's voice cuts through the moment. "Is there any place she can stay tonight? Our hotel is surrounded by paparazzi, and she really doesn't want to be seen." *Especially with you* is the unspoken addendum to that statement, but it doesn't throw me. I've been snuck in and out of plenty of hotels. None in Sydney yet, so that's a kookaburra feather in a cap or something.

Asta's gaze quickly glides from Nora to me. There's a question there, but she's far too professional to let it show. "Of course. We have a few rooms reserved for guests who prefer to stay overnight. If you need a change of clothes, our shop is open. Or perhaps we could send someone out shopping for you tomorrow."

How I would love to take Nora shopping at the L+L store. There's a bustier she would look fabulous in that's a lot easier to move in than one would think. Not that I have personal experience with that or anything.

Nora's shoulders relax an inch. "Yes. Thank you. That would be great."

"Excellent. Ludo, you can use the Blue Room. It should suit your needs. Do you know where it is?"

"Absolutely." Perfect. As far as the rooms here go, it's relatively non-threatening, and Nora looks like she could use something easy.

"Very well." Asta gathers all the paperwork and turns to Nora. "Thank you so much for attending. I hope we will see you again."

Nora doesn't reply but nods.

Billie wraps an arm around her shoulders and squeezes. "I'm off, too, okay? You're going to have a great time."

A moment of panic flees across Nora's expression. I mean, I'm not *that* bad. Most of the time. Unless someone wants me to be.

The moment passes quickly, and her features behind her mask settle into that uber-sexy look of determination. "I'll be all right. Thanks, Billie. Really."

"Anything for you, babe." Billie's eyes tear up and she pulls her friend into a deep hug. "You deserve this. Have the *best* time."

What is going on here? She's acting like Nora's on Rumspringa or something. Not my place. Not my place. I am Ludo-not-Luke, sex worker, fake boyfriend for the week. Soon to be debt-free. That's more than enough for me not to pry into whatever this situation is.

Billie heads out, catching more than a few interested glances on her way out.

"Well, my lady, it's just you and me." I hold out a hand to her. "Can I show you to the room?"

Nora pauses, her posture erect and perfect. Maybe she's a dancer. Or some sort of influencer, but she'd have to be extra famous for her to be able to drop five hundred thousand dollars at a glance. I can't wait to get that mask off her.

No. Not my place.

I really need to cut off my curiosity. "Look. I know this is a little weird, right? It's not every day you get to spend a week with an amazing guy who will cater to your every whim."

It was the right thing to say. The tight lines around her eyes soften infinitesimally. So I push my luck. I have to. I *need* that money. So badly I can almost taste it. And it will probably taste like blood and teeth once Tobias finds me.

I put my hand in my pocket and lean closer to her, so it's just us. Me and Nora. This is what I'm good at, and I wouldn't do this for anyone, but she seems...nice. So I drop the Australian accent.

"My name's Luke. I'm from Menomonee Falls, Wisconsin. I'm not a serial killer. Your best friend is awesome and clearly adores you, and that makes me like you, too. I don't know who you are or what brought you here, but this week is about you. What you need, what you want. Nothing will happen that you do not explicitly agree to. I'm not into that, and my boss would kill me."

Nora's eyebrow sweeps upward. "That's probably true. She's incredible."

My powers of reading people have won again. "Yes, she is."

Nora stares at her empty glass. "Luke, huh? You're American?"

"Yeah. When I first started this job in Spain, Ludo went over better. I can be a lot of things to a lot of people." I shrug, like it's no big deal, but at the time giving up Luke for Ludo had felt like climbing the Eiger. But I needed a change. I needed not to be me.

The statement seems to catch her, and her eyebrow twitches over the rim of her mask. "Who will you be to me?"

I soften a bit. "A friend."

She nods, as if in approval. "Wisconsin? Do you have family? Pets?"

I don't have a ton of rules, but I typically don't reveal a lot about my actual self. Less complicated that way. Still, Nora is different and I'm desperate. If this is what she needs so I can get my money, done. My mom will forgive me. "My mom. Two cats. We didn't eat that much cheese when I was growing up. I'm lactose intolerant."

She processes this information slowly, like she's writing it into her brain. It's strangely attentive. No one else I've been with has taken so much care about me. It's usually all about them.

"Okay," she says. "Show me the Blue Room."

CHAPTER 9

ora

I KEEP my gaze straight ahead and my mask on as we walk down one of the hallways that sprout like electrical cords from the main stage area. My heart beats so quickly I can hear it like a herd of wildebeest in my ears.

"Hey, this isn't the voyeur hall. No need to worry." Luke's smile is easy and soft, but I can't manage to meet it.

This is a mistake. My parents won't find the bank transfer, because I used my private account. But what happens when I'm not in my hotel room tomorrow morning? They raised hell the day after my date with Jayden. I only just got rid of the 24/7 security detail last week. Even worse, what happens when I take off the mask? People have all sorts of reactions to meeting me, but the one that always weighs me down is Expectations. What are Luke's expectations of the Purity Pledge Princess?

Luke stops before a door and keys in a code. The light blinks green twice, and he pushes it open.

Impossibly, my heart beats even faster. Maybe there's a defibrillator around here somewhere.

There's definitely only one bed.

I'm not sure why I expected something different. The rest of the room doesn't look like a dungeon or anything. It's clean and cool with teal-colored walls and no windows. There is a chair in the corner and a swing hanging from one of the rafters.

A blue room built for sin.

You're built for sin but you took a vow to be chaste. Should I test that vow?

Ugh, Pastor Curt. I push all memories of that dickhead way back to the far recesses of my brain. He deserves none of my time and has no place here.

Luke walks into the room and removes his mask. Despite my racing heartbeat, my mouth waters. Talk about sin. With the mask on, he is gorgeous, but without it? His skin is a light golden brown and his eyes sparkle, like he is always ready to play. He's beautiful. "Do you want anything to drink or—"

"I'm a virgin."

Oops. I hadn't meant to say that out loud. Smooth, Nora, real smooth.

I stick my hands into the front pocket of my hoodie and rock backward on my heels. To his credit, Luke runs a hand through his hair, loosening the strands. It's almost like the wind through prairie grass, if prairie grass were sexy. Which it's not.

I am such a mess. And I'm not referring to my song, "Hot Mess." My parents *hate* that song. It's the last one they allowed me to write.

"Okay," he says. There's no judgment or bias implied, no shock. It's a simple statement of fact.

"Okay?" I can't keep the astonishment from my tone. Only Billie has ever been this understanding.

He shrugs. "It's your body. Do what you want with it. Do you want something to drink?"

The aftereffects of the alcohol are making me feel lethargic and woozy, like this is all a dream and I'll wake up in my hotel room with my mom and a dozen wedding dresses I had no say in selecting. On second thought, I'd rather be here in the dream. "Sure. Thank you."

Turning, he opens the door of a mini fridge and pulls out two bottles of water. He hands one to me. The cool of the plastic soothes my palms, which are fiery hot for some reason. "I mean, the entire idea of virginity is really a patriarchal concept, designed—"

"—designed to reinforce feudal systems and consolidate power," I interject. I can't help myself. It's so rare I find someone else who feels this way. It's part of the reason Billie and I became friends.

"Exactly." Luke holds my gaze for a single, searing moment before cracking open his bottled water and sipping it. "Don't even get me started about the hymen."

My heart has stopped its thoroughbred pacing and now leaps in my chest like a kid at a trampoline park. "Do you think a lot about the hymen?" I don't even think I've said that word aloud in a long time. It's freeing, not to have to censor my thoughts.

"It's a job hazard."

Oh. Right. We aren't two friends chatting about the patriarchy over bottled water. He is a sex worker whom I hired to deflower me.

My hands still. "You must think I'm ridiculous."

"No." He places the water on a table and walks toward me. "I think you're beautiful and mysterious."

A sharp laugh breaks from me. "Mysterious? Sometimes

it feels like everyone knows who I am except for me." Where I am, what I'm doing, who I'm with, who I'm wearing, what I said when I was tired and hungry and just wanted to get the fuck out of there. Every mistake, catalogued on social media for eternity.

But now Luke is so close, inches away from me. He's sexy and sweet and right here. This is what I want, isn't it?

"Can I touch you?" I ask.

"Sure." He shrugs again, a tic that seems almost a routine for him, like he brushes away any discomfort with a simple lift of his shoulders.

Broad shoulders. But not too broad. I've met guys who work out constantly who have definition even in the tiny angles of their neck muscles, but Luke is… pleasantly buff.

I run my hands over the smooth front of his flight attendant's uniform, the sleek silkiness of the fabric gliding against my fingertips. There's hard warmth beneath the shirt, and Luke smells amazing. Like musk and cinnamon and clean linen. I want to ball my hands in the shirt, pull him closer, and drown in this scent.

Luke doesn't touch me, but he inhales sharply as I continue my chaste over-the-shirt exploration. "Can I take off your mask?"

My hands still as if of their own accord. Everything will change if I take off the mask. It protects me. I am simply Nora here, and I haven't been allowed to be her in so very, very long. As I look up into Luke's eyes, there's no judgment. Curiosity, yes. Heat, yes. But he doesn't act on any of it. Mr. Sex on a Stick is holding himself back, to make me comfortable.

It's wildly hot. The least I can do is be honest with him.

I reach behind my head and pull on the elastic strap holding the mask in place. It slides off my face far too quickly, and I shiver. Exposed.

A soft smile spreads across Luke's face. He reaches toward me but doesn't touch, his fingertips gliding over the air two centimeters from my skin. Like he's tracing my features, or painting them. "You're beautiful, Nora."

Wait a minute. The genuine use of the name I gave him, the lack of surprise or widened eyes.

Does he not know who I am?

A flush of irritation works itself through me, followed quickly by the warm, sinuous heat of pleasure. Despite the fact that I am internationally famous—I mean, I was the Super Bowl halftime show last year—here is a man who does not seem to know who I am.

It's wonderful. How this is my luck completely escapes me, but I'll take the win. This one win. Maybe fate is finally on my side.

"May I kiss you?" I ask as my neck erupts in an unpleasant and unsexy blush. "Or wait. Is that something you don't do? I've seen *Pretty Woman*."

His brown eyes deepen, like they're the heart at the center of a bonfire. "I thought you'd never ask."

His body presses against mine, flooding me with *him*. His heat, his smell, all hard lines and smooth fabric. With his hands, he cups my face and bends down to close the last few centimeters between us, and it is connection and fire. It lifts me up and surrounds me. Within the first second of our lips meeting, I'm certain this is the best kiss I have ever had or ever will.

Rational thought quickly retreats to the far corners of my tired, over-worked brain. *Luke.* I wrap my arms around his neck, pulling him closer, turning my head to deepen the kiss.

He doesn't push, just continues the slow, sensuous licks and suckles and rubbing. How are his lips so soft? How does his breath taste so good? How is it that when he kisses me like this, without tongue or pushing it too far or trying to cop a feel, I feel simultaneously naked and powerful?

He presses me against the wall and one of his hands drops to my waist, pulling me closer to him. I want more and also like there is never enough. I'm supported, buoyed by him and bolstered by the wall, so I can give in to the headiness of this kiss. I am ethereal, floating above, watching myself make out with this gorgeous man and thinking *get it, girl.*

He breaks the kiss and I come up for air, swollen and needy and lightheaded.

"That was—" I start to say.

He kisses me gently—on the lips, above the arch of my eyebrows, on the ridge of my temples. Each touch sears my skin. "It's been a long day. Let's get some sleep."

"Sleep?" It's almost like he told me this was all a dream, and now I have to go back and marry some stranger like my parents want. "I don't want to sleep."

He laughs lightly, but I can feel how he wants me. I'm a virgin but I'm not totally naive.

"I want to have sex," I say, but my voice flounders and the whole effect is dampened by an unsexy yawn. It's impossible to seduce someone when yawning. Did he kiss me into some weird form of submission?

He steps away, one hand still holding my waist, like he isn't fully ready to break the touch between us. "There's time. We're both tired. Let's talk more tomorrow."

Part of me wants to protest, wants to get this whole thing over with. I made this plan, I need to execute it, and my courage only extends so far.

But then there's the part of me that yawns like a sleepy kitten. I've spent the last eight years of my life constantly on the move, and for the first time in that almost-decade, I don't have a minute-by-minute agenda for my day tomorrow.

There's only one thing on my to do list, and he's standing in front of me, fully clothed, telling me there's time.

It's refreshing.

"But there's only the one bed." I point at it. No black silk sheets, just clean white linens and thick fluffy pillows. There is also an enormous mirror on the ceiling and covering one wall. Maybe that's the kinky part of this, or maybe they really do reserve the Blue Room for overnight guests. I don't know and I don't particularly care. I'm glad it's here. I'm glad we are here.

Dragging his fingertips from my waist, he runs his other hand through his hair. "I can sleep on the chair, if you like."

Right. I chew on the inside of my cheek, the ridge of flesh hard where I bite it constantly. "I think I'd like to sleep next to you, if you are okay with that."

Something cozy and surprised flashes through his eyes. "Sure. Okay."

"Right." I feel like an asshole. A very large part of me wants to go back to the kissing that put me into such a sleepy mood, but maybe that's the adrenaline withdrawal, too. "Great. Tomorrow."

CHAPTER 10

uke

ALL I HAVE ARE questions and a massive erection that's making it hard to think of potential, non-threatening ways to ask any of the questions.

I shouldn't have slept beside Nora. Huge mistake. Huge. It hadn't seemed an issue last night when we were both exhausted. But that kiss? I didn't know what to expect. I have kissed a lot of women and men, and everyone is a little bit different. But Nora? Nora kissed me like she was hungry for me, like she wouldn't stop until she had explored every part of me, in and out. She kissed me like she had always been denied candy and I was her very first Life Saver. Cherry flavored.

None of this helps with my erection issue.

In the bed, I shift slightly away from her. I've had plenty of practice sneaking out of beds in the morning, don't get me wrong, but I don't want to wake her. She's... serene.

Adorable. She didn't take her hair out of the bun last night so a giant mass of hair flops over her head like a misshapen bobblehead. One arm is flung over her face, hiding her from the world.

Why does a woman like her need to hide?

My cock throbs harder. I could wake her. She said this is what she wants, but as much as I can be a witless asshole, I'm not a complete dickhead. No woman wants to lose her virginity just because some douche-nozzle has morning wood.

Besides, Nora is…special.

And mysterious. That thought alone should be enough to tell my cock to stand down. A mystery woman with five hundred grand and one v card to burn is not someone I should think is special.

It doesn't help.

I slide out of bed and sneak into the en-suite bathroom, which has a massive shower and a full-length mirror across from it. The Blue Room is usually reserved for people who want to watch themselves having sex, which is a kink I fully enjoy on a routine day.

This time, I don't want an audience, not even an audience of one, while I jerk off. It's a cold shower and the visual imprint of Nora in those skin tight gray leggings for me.

Twenty minutes and one orgasm of self-loathing later, I lean against the wall of the bathroom and sigh. I need a plan. One that involves keeping Nora interested so she doesn't request a refund but also one that gives me space to deal with the very physical consequences of spending so much time with her.

As if on cue, Nora knocks rapidly on the closed door. "Um, Luke?"

"Yeah?" She can't tell I've been whacking off in here, right? That would be the very definition of uncomfortable.

"Is there a back way out of this place?"

Hm. A curious turn in the conversation, but I can roll with it. I open the door and lean against the jamb, affecting full nonchalance in a way that I hope telegraphs *there's absolutely no way I was jerking off in here while thinking about sleeping next to you.* She looks gorgeous awake, her mascara blurred and her hair tousled. It almost looks like she's been fucked, but I mean, I've been here, so…

Her expression halts my thoughts.

"Why do you look nervous?" My skin prickles with a sense of impending dread.

Her gaze darts to the door then back to me. "Your boss called. Asta? She said some people are waiting outside." A pleading tone enters her voice. "I—I can't be seen. Can we get out of here?"

Every muscle in my body tenses and every nerve surges to high alert. People waiting. Fuck. Tobias found me. I can't let them find Nora. Come to think of it, if we stay anywhere here in Sydney, he'll find me. Suddenly this town feels very small. "Don't worry. This is a sex club, Nora. It's all discreet back exits."

ora

HE DRESSES with such astonishing alacrity that I wonder if maybe he does know who I am. Maybe he realized it last night when we were sleeping. I also don't know why the fuck I care, because I need to get out of here.

They'll follow me. My parents and the bodyguards they inevitably hired. They must have tracked my phone. The minute we get somewhere I can use my hands, I'm disabling all location services. I'll get cash somehow instead of using my credit cards.

I know Luke is not a long-term solution to my problem, but this is my chance. My week. Last night was the single best night of sleep I've had in eight years, and it's because I made my own damned choices regarding my body and I have zero expectations of me today. My mother isn't about to swan into my hotel room and not-so-subtly deride how late I want to sleep in. My manager isn't going to side-eye my breakfast choices, then make some asinine remark about how he'll need to talk to my stylist if I keep eating whole eggs instead of egg whites.

It's impossible to spend too much time on this when running from either paparazzi or a private investigator.

I run beside Luke down a hallway and he opens a door at the end, leading to a well-lit staircase. "Thank you," I say, panting a little though this is hardly my usual cardio routine. "I really appreciate you doing this."

"No problem." There's something in his tone that would make me pause if I didn't desperately need to escape. Is someone after him, too?

I shrug it off as we jump the last few stairs and Luke opens the door onto a deserted alleyway with a parking garage a few meters away. I glance around quickly, but there's no one here. I'm not sure where Asta had seen the people she called me to report, yet I'm immensely grateful to her.

Luke is still holding my hand, and for the first time, I realize how pleasant it is. His skin is warm but not sweaty or clammy. He must have showered, so he smells clean and fresh, with an undertone of cinnamon.

I like it.

We dash across the street just as two people who are not dressed for the early morning chill round the corner and shout to us.

Shit.

Grateful I wore my sneakers on this poorly-thought-out mission, I outpace Luke, crossing through streets and ducking down a random assortment of alleyways. This always happens to me when I run. The whole world fades except the smack of my sneakers against the pavement, the rush of wind in my ears, the burn in my chest. All the shit I deal with on a daily basis takes a back seat in my brain and I feel free and unencumbered.

I wish there were something else in the world that makes me feel like this.

"Nora, slow down." Luke's voice hitches with a sound like pain, breaking into my runner's reverie, and I slow, panting, my breath searing through my chest like acid. "I think we've lost them."

Hands on my hips, I turn, but it's not like I have any idea where we are. I've been to Sydney before, but only in the sense of being whisked from one enclosed area to another. There are buildings here but they could be buildings in any city in the world. Gray, nondescript monstrosities.

I'd turn on my phone but I've already vowed to disable all the location services, which means maps are out.

Luke, though, has his in his hand and he's typing with the assurance of someone who does this all the time. "How do you feel about Perth?"

What kind of a question is that? "I don't know. Neutral? Look, Luke, we need to get out of here. I don't know where we are—"

"It's cool." He holds up his screen which has a ride share app pulled up on it. "Driver in five. What do you think about Perth?"

I hate how he's completely blasé about this. His tone, like I should know exactly what he's talking about, irks me almost as much as being told I am to marry a stranger. I cross my arms over my chest. "I'm still lost. Metaphorically and literally speaking."

"Right." He laughs a little, and a lock of brown hair falls over his forehead. It's boyish and adorable and I should not want to sweep it off his brow. "Sorry. Of course you don't have a window into my weird brain. I have this pilot friend, and he says he can take us to Perth if we can get to the private jet terminal in thirty minutes."

"Oh." He actually thought up a plan and executed it while he was running away from the paparazzi? Unless there are people chasing him, too, and why exactly do I think flying to Perth is a good idea? Then again, is it a good idea to spend half a million dollars on a man to fuck me out of my virginity curse? Sorry, "Purity Pledge." It definitely didn't feel like a curse when I believed what my parents do, but eight years can change a person.

It's not like I can say any of this to him.

"Why Perth?" I ask instead.

"It's one of the most remote cities in the world. It's supposed to be lovely. Right on the Swan River." He sticks his hands into the pockets of his flight attendant's uniform, which is strangely unwrinkled. Wait, did he sleep in his boxers last night after I passed out and I missed it? Damn my poor alcohol tolerance. Not the time, Nora. "Plus, it's a free ride out of Sydney." He nods toward the path I suppose we've traveled. "It seems like you need to get out of here."

He doesn't ask why, which I appreciate. I'm not ready to admit about Honora Grand if he hasn't figured it out for himself. With my luck, we'll pass by the billboard with my massive face on it on the way to the airport, and then the jig is up anyway.

He's also not admitting that he ran very quickly without knowing why. Before I get on a plane with him to "the most remote city in the world," maybe I should clarify a few things.

"Who are you running from?" I ask.

He shifts from foot to foot. "I'm not."

"You ran pretty fast without knowing why or who you were running from. Are you in trouble? Are you a serial killer?" Thank God Billie took a picture of his drivers' license. "Are you taking me to Perth to feed me to dingoes?"

He barks a surprised laugh as a trim little white sedan pulls up beside us. "That was quite a leap. Look, I'm not a serial killer. I'm not a criminal. I've made some choices for very good reasons which have had... unintended consequences. But there is no way in this or any world that I would put you in danger. I promise."

A promise. People have made me a lot of promises. Has anyone ever kept them?

A small car turns down the road and stops in front of us. With a flourish and a hopeful look on his face, he opens the door to the sedan. "Your carriage, my lady?"

I should not get in this car. I should go back to the hotel and return to what I knew before. My family and Marvin steamrolling my life, all in the name of "what's good for me." It's gotten me this far, hasn't it? Money, fame, people who rush to fix an eyebrow emergency?

What girl wouldn't trade a few freedoms for all of that?

The ride share driver leans over the back of the front seat and looks at us. "If we wait any longer, I'm charging another fiver."

Luke stares at me, not like he wants something from me, but like he wants to help. Like he could be a friend. I told him what I needed him for, and he's treating me the way I've always secretly hoped someone would. Taking it slow, making me feel important, not just a challenge. I'm not a white rhino, prey for a dentist on a safari vacation. At my core, I am always just Nora.

I slide into the car, keeping my sunglasses firmly in place. "This conversation isn't over."

uke

THANK GOODNESS FOR GILES. He doesn't even question when we arrive five minutes before he's supposed to leave. He pulls me in for a hug, his dark brown curls tamed with a heavy amount of pomade. "Hey, mate. How's it?"

"All right. Thanks for taking us." I take Nora's hand and drag her forward. She has a shy sort of smile on her face, and she still hasn't taken off her sunglasses. "This is Nora."

"Nora. Hi." Giles extends a hand toward her, his white pilot's shirt perfectly buttoned to his dark brown wrist. Nora shakes it firmly. "No luggage, eh? What are you two doing in Perth?"

Beside me, Nora stiffens, so I search my brain for any possible thing we could do or that I know about the city. Honestly, what I know about Perth could fill the eye of a needle. Damn the public school system.

"Seeing the quokka," Nora says quietly.

I'm not sure if it's what she says or the timbre of her voice, but Giles's eyes widen a couple of centimeters. Does he know who she is? Before I can ask, he says, "Cool. Right on. They're very cute, the quokka."

How does everyone know what this is and should I google it before we take off?

But just as quickly as Giles reacted, he wipes his expression clean. "Wheels up in ten. If you need the loo or anything, there's one on board or you can use the one there for crew." He gestures toward a door very clearly marked as a restroom. He hits me on the shoulder, a little harder than usual. "If you need anything, you know how to call."

"Right." I rub at my joint as he disappears into the cabin.

"Is he the only pilot?" Nora asks, scraping her palms against her leggings. Her thighs are almost obscenely toned, long and pretty. She must spend hours a day running or dancing. I'm not here to look or covet. I'm here to do a job. Even if that job still has her hair up in a messy bun and her sunglasses in place, which make her look incredibly and eminently kissable.

My cock throbs, but I think again of what the fuck a quokka could be—an STD? A famous leper colony?—and it subsides.

"Yeah. It's a repositioning flight, so they don't need a full crew." I gesture toward the gangplank, and follow her onboard the private jet, definitely not looking at the perfect round peach of her ass. I wonder if the designers of the emoji used Nora's ass as a model. Maybe that's how she made her money. "Do you need ibuprofen or anything?"

"What?" She slides into one of the captain's chairs beside the front windows and removes her sunglasses. Her eyes are almost emerald in the faint strains of morning light streaming in through the window.

Next thing I know, I'll be waxing rhapsodic or some shit.

I need to get myself together. This is a job. I am Ludo, romance and sexpert. Not some lovesick Victorian with tuberculosis and ink stains on my fingers.

As I take two bottles of water from the galley fridge, I nod toward her sunglasses. "You were wearing those all morning. I wasn't sure if you were hungover." I hand her a bottle of water, then head back for the galley so I can surreptitiously take three ibuprofen. My back is killing me. "I could make you a drink, too, if you like. A little hair of the dog. I make a mean mai tai or a dirty blonde."

"What's that?" She untwists the cap, and with that simple, assured gesture, I'm hard again. It's just a water bottle, for chrissakes.

"It's a—" the idea of explaining why I know my boss's favorite drink and thereby informing her that I am a giant kiss-ass, is not appealing —"never mind."

"Okay." She stares out the window and settles back in her seat, phone in her hand.

"Are you googling what a quokka is?" I apparently cannot control my desire to hear her smoky-sugary voice again.

She smirks, the twist of her mouth a shockingly intoxicating sight. "I already know what it is."

"Cheeky."

Her gaze flicks to mine, and she holds it there, like she's in charge and she likes it that way. Same. It's been a while since I've seduced someone without experience, but I feel like this is a good start. Let her be in charge and dictate what happens. I'll make no demands. Unless she decides she likes that, too.

My cock is not going to survive this kind of rumination, so I buckle my seatbelt and take out my phone. Asta has already wired ten percent of my fee for this week to my bank account. I'll get the rest at the end of the seven days.

Perfect timing. I immediately set up a bank transfer to

pay my mom's hospital bills. Tobias can wait until the deadline, but my mom can't.

My phone pings with a notification from an unknown number, requesting to air drop a file to my phone. A small kernel of dread coils deep in my stomach. Tobias couldn't possibly know I'm here, right? I disabled my location services after the ride share dropped us off here at the terminal.

But I can't ignore it. If it is him, maybe I'll explain that he'll get everything I owe, despite his lack of faith in me.

So it's a massive surprise when I open the notification and instead of an angry demand for more money, it's a video. A video of a small, gopher-like animal with brown fur and a roly-poly body. It's smiling. Really, actually smiling. I watch the whole thing three times before Nora laughs softly beside me.

"It's a quokka." Smiling, she settles back into her captain's chair and closes her eyes. "You're welcome."

CHAPTER 13

ora

"You know, this is not the wildest first date I've ever been on." Luke stands at the galley, fixing some sort of egg bake for the three of us that smells incredible. I hadn't realized how hungry I was, but I'm grateful the roar of the engines drowns out the rumble of my stomach.

"Really?" I watch him from my seat, completely ignoring the sight of Sydney disappearing below us as we soar toward the clouds.

"Oh yeah." He hands me eggs and an oat milk latte with a sprinkle of cinnamon and the foam curled into the shape of a sun. "The wildest involves a bullfight and an emu named Harry."

I laugh so hard I almost spill his latte creation. "I'll bet you have all kinds of stories."

"Oh yeah." He knocks on the door to the cabin, and hands Giles his breakfast before returning to me and settling into

63

the opposite seat. He sighs with pleasure as he shakes his white cloth napkin over his lap. "Nothing like running for your life to work up an appetite." His brown eyes twinkle as they catch the sunlight from my window. "Unless we're talking sex."

Like I would know. I take a bite of my breakfast, which is a rich and creamy red pepper and chicken sausage thing with caramelized onions. "This tastes amazing. I can't believe you made all this in an airplane kitchen."

Luke shrugs and pops a bite of egg into his mouth. "I've had a lot of practice. Lots of odd jobs before I settled in full time at Leather and Lace. Working at a cafe was my favorite."

I sip at the latte and moan with pleasure as the spicy sweet warmth rolls through me. "I don't think I've ever tasted anything like this. You're a coffee genius."

"Thanks." His pleasure is genuine. I spend enough time around people who bullshit professionally, and I've gotten pretty good at spotting it. This? Luke really likes making coffee drinks. It's a glimpse behind the curtain. Super sexy and also artistic. "It's part of why I moved here, to Australia. I wanted to learn more about their coffee scene. I also just like trying on places."

"Are you going to open a coffee shop?" I savor the latte, not wanting it to be gone too soon. Hell, I'm going to savor every moment of this week, this unexpected gift.

"I don't know. I haven't really thought about it." He sets to his meal, which means he definitely has thought about it and doesn't want to discuss it. That's fine. We have time.

We finish our breakfast in relative silence, the only sound soft music piped in through the speakers. I recognize The Waifs, Crowded House, Iggy Azalea. It's not until the opening strains of my song "Believe Me" come on that I ask if Luke can turn down the music.

He doesn't seem to register the connection, and my

shoulders slump in relief. I don't know what rock in the Outback he's been living under, but I'm sending it a commemorative plaque.

"What about you?" He clears my empty plate and utensils, but I hold onto my coffee. The sun symbol has faded by this point, but this latte is still the best thing I've ever tasted. "What was your wildest date?"

I laugh, not fully intending to do so, but it's out there now. "I don't really date."

His eyes widen in disbelief. "Are you kidding? You're gorgeous."

Hmm. How to tread carefully without admitting who I am? "When I was younger, my parents refused to allow me to date. They said I was too young."

"But you're, what? Twenty-three, twenty-four?"

I sigh and stare out the window, the latte warming my palms. "Suffice it to say, they still don't let me date. I've had one boyfriend but we were rarely alone." And could he even really be called my boyfriend? He was a member of my parents' church who wanted to get into music production. At the time, I thought he'd liked me for me, but I wasn't quite as wise as I am now.

He finishes cleaning the plates and returns again to his seat, wiping his hands dry. "Not to be indelicate, but is that why you're a virgin? And—I'm asking in a professional capacity here, so if you don't want to answer, that's fine— exactly what kind of virgin are you?"

I sip my latte as my stomach twists. Oddly, the creamy coffee soothes me. "Are there different kinds? Or are you asking if I've had any experience?"

"The latter. Though again, this is all about you. If you don't feel comfortable talking about it, I respect that."

I've reached the end of my latte. Shame. "If I can't talk about sex, I shouldn't be having it, right? Okay, I've—I've almost given a hand job before, but that's about it." Thoughts of Pastor Curt and his wandering hands threaten to intrude into the moment, but the oat milk latte grounds me. Magic coffee.

The lines of Luke's jaw tighten, like he knows what I'm not saying. It's oddly endearing, this protective quality.

My cheeks flush. "Like I said, my life has not always been my own. A well-timed knee in the groin is a good skill to have."

"That really sucks, Nora. I'm sorry." There's warmth and trust and honesty in his voice. It reminds me of his latte.

I brush it off, but it sticks to me like dog hair. Never got to have a dog, either. "It happens. People can be giant assholes." Tears prickle at the backs of my eyes, but I push them away.

"You don't have to brush it off. Whatever that dickhead did, none of it was your fault." Luke reaches across the aisle between us and takes my hand in his. "So, tell me what your perfect date would be, if you could have anything you wanted."

His palm against mine, our fingers twisted together. It feels...nice. Comfortable. A little like home. "Anything I want?"

He squeezes my hand gently, and a tingle of pleasure zings up my arm. "Anything."

I bite my lip, close my eyes, and allow myself to dream. I don't need to dig deep for this fantasy. "It would be just us, me and him. We'd go to some quiet little bar, some place with live music. It would be a little dingy, the acoustics okay but not amazing. The floor smells like old beer and stale fries, but it's warm inside and the people are friendly. Nobody talks to us except the waitress who takes our order. It's open mic night. A kid gets up on stage and blows us all away, their voice like angels singing us to heaven and back. Maybe we get a little drunk. Maybe we eat too much. Our hands hurt from clapping so hard and our throats ache from cheering for this kid. Then we'd go home, back to a little house, maybe on the water somewhere. Someplace away and quiet that belonged only to us." I swallow, my throat dry as chalk. "That would be my perfect date."

Luke is silent as he watches me, his hand tight against mine. "That is amazing."

"There's a bar like that in Nashville," I say. I can tell him this. He won't make the association. "I sang there once, when I was younger."

"That sounds like a good memory." He clears his throat. "Do you like to sing?"

I pull my hand from his and stare out the window, but there's only clouds there now. "I used to love it."

uke

I WAKE with a startle as the wheels of the plane hit the ground and the cabin shudders, but only for a moment.

"That was the smoothest landing I've had in a while," Nora says. I glance over at her, and she's absorbed in an old issue of *Vanity Fair* with Bobby Nakamura, first baseman for Milwaukee, on the cover.

"Giles is an awesome pilot." I yawn and stretch, the bottom hem of my T-shirt riding up my abs. "One time, I got him drunk and he told me all these wild stories about the shit he used to pull. He was a rescue pilot on K2 for a while, and he flew planes in Afghanistan before that."

Nora turns to me, her eyes wide. "Wow. That's cool."

"He's a very chatty drunk." I yawn again. There isn't time to make coffee as we taxi toward the terminal, but this is Oz. I'm sure I can find a cafe somewhere.

"Have you thought at all about where we might stay?"

Nora folds the magazine into her lap. "No pressure or anything."

"Right." I pull out my phone and flip it off airplane mode. We'll need supplies, clothes, food. Might as well order those when I book a place. "What do you like? Maybe a hotel?" Nora seems like she is used to five star resorts, but even with the cash from the auction, I'm not sure I can afford a week of such luxury.

"No." She answers too quickly. "Somewhere private, small. I don't need much."

She means it, too. She might have dropped half a million on a week with me—which, believe me, she'll get her money's worth—but then she sits there in her cozy leggings and her sweatshirt with little holes at the cuffs where she's worn through the stitching. And that story? About her perfect date? Adorable.

I spend the remainder of the time before we reach the terminal searching through vacation rental bookings, and find the perfect spot. Okay, not perfect but more than serviceable. It's a little south of Perth's central business district, located in Fremantle, but it will be quiet. In minutes, I book and pay with my credit card. I doubt Tobias is really looking into my credit history. He's more of a rough-em-up type of investigator rather than a forensic accountant. I'm safe for now.

I take a few moments and send twenty grand to Tobias's account. It's all I have left of my advance for now, but hopefully it will buy me some time. Finally. A little twist of fate and things are looking up. Thank you, mystery Nora.

"Folks, we are here in lovely Perth," Giles says over the plane's cabin loudspeaker. I don't know what's up with him today, but he keeps trying to play the same pop songs over and over. Every single time he does, Nora goes pale as a sheet. It's like a bizarre Pavlovian response. "Please keep your seatbelts fastened and pull your damned pants back on. Cheers." Ah, Giles. He's flown a couple of times for Leather and Lace Travel, so he knows his audience. Except Nora isn't exactly the typical client.

Nora laughs lightly, though there's a flush in her cheeks. "What does he think we've been doing?"

"No comment." My reply is too quick. I forgot to make it casual, charming, off the cuff, and she's caught that, because she's staring at me like I've suddenly become the most fascinating person in the room. Fucking perfect.

She stares out the window, and I start to relax. "I'll bet you see a lot, in your job."

My shoulders relax another inch, and I flip to a local delivery app to arrange for toiletries and changes of clothes to be delivered to the holiday house. "Yeah. I don't yuck anyone's yum, but I'll say that some people are…entitled, to say the least."

She harrumphs as though she has also had experience with this. She probably has. Whoever she was talking about who she almost gave a hand job to is right up there on my shit list.

My hands tighten into fists, the pressure so strong they go numb. I really, really hate bullies who try to take advantage. No woman should have to learn self-defense simply to live her life.

The plane rolls into a berth at the terminal, and I get up from my seat to help Giles with the disembarkation procedures. It's rote work at this point, which is good. I need to take my mind off Nora. I need to remember my role here. I might be playing her boyfriend, but she's not interested in the real Luke. She doesn't want to know about my mom or my hometown or Tobias. This is her fantasy and I'm a part of it. If I don't play that role, all that beautiful, life-changing money will go up in smoke.

"You're being remarkably quiet," I say to Giles, mostly to dull the inner conversation that keeps reminding me what a lovely intrigue Nora is.

"Me? Hardly." He glances over his shoulder as the staircase lowers down from the side of the plane. "Take care of yourself, mate." He clasps my shoulder, too hard, like he's not going to let me go. I cannot, in fact, get out of his grasp.

Nora stands and disembarks slowly, her movements ballerina-light. "Is there a bathroom in the terminal?"

"Absolutely. Enjoy Perth." Giles tilts his hat toward her with one hand, but with the other squeezes my shoulder so tightly I think he's about to dislocate it.

I wait until Nora is out of sight before wrenching away from Giles's grasp, massaging sensation back into my shoulder. "What the fuck, man? I could have nerve damage."

Giles's expression isn't contrite, the asshole. His eyes gleam like he's an archaeologist who's finally found his long lost treasure. "Are you kidding me, Luke?"

"No. My shoulder fucking hurts."

He grabs me again, slightly gentler this time, and turns me in the direction Nora took when she left. "You don't know who she is?"

"She's Nora. Nora Grandin." That's what she's told me, and that's what I'm sticking to.

Giles shakes his head violently, but his well-fitting pilot's cap doesn't move. "No, mate. You really need to pay more attention to pop culture. Didn't you hear those songs I kept playing? That's Honora Fucking Grand."

It feels like a lightbulb has exploded inside my brain, embedding little shards of glass into every neuron in my body. Honora Grand. I might not listen to pop music or pay much attention to entertainment—I'm too busy working— but even I have heard of her. Pop's Perfect Princess with her Purity Pledge and her evangelical background. Isn't there a rumor about her manager being part of a Christian Mafia thing?

And she's hired me, Luke Bautista, sex worker and flight attendant, to take her virginity.

"Fucking perfect," I growl under my breath. How the hell am I supposed to do this? No wonder she wants her privacy. If her parents find out, I'm not just dead, I'm disappeared, wiped from the face of this earth. Erased from the internet, even. What will my mom say?

Giles whistles at my expression, which must be a weird constellation of confused and furious. "What in the world are you doing with Honora Grand, Luke?"

What indeed?

A thousand things snap into place, and I grab Giles by his shoulder, exerting the same amount of pressure he gave to me. I'll do anything—*anything*—to preserve her anonymity so we can finish out this week. Giles is just going to have to roll with that.

"No one can know. You can't say anything. Do you understand me?"

CHAPTER 15

ora

LUKE CALLS a ride share from the airport to take us to the home rental he's found. It's peaceful in the back of the car, despite the volume of the driver's music and the overly pungent air freshener. Regardless, I can breathe here.

Raindrops trickle down the windows, and I trace them with my fingertips.

"It's barmy, it is," the driver says. "Normally we get over one hundred and forty days of sunshine, and you poor folks show up during the gloom."

"I don't mind." I lean against the window, the pane cool against my skin. I'd rather lean against Luke. His warmth is magnetic, but I don't think he'd appreciate that. "I've always liked the rain."

"Not me. Give me the sun any day." Luke stretches out his legs beside me. He's been acting oddly ever since we landed. I hope he isn't upset that I asked him to arrange everything and pay for the vacation rental. He's been so understanding about how reticent I am about my past, and I appreciate it immensely.

"I can pay you back, for the rental," I say quietly.

His eyes widen in surprise and he shakes his head. "Don't worry about it. It's my pleasure."

In the distance there's a huge torus-shaped stadium, almost indistinguishable to me from all the other ones I've played over the years.

"That's where our cricket team plays," the driver explains, pointing. "Third largest in Oz. You can do a tour there if you like. You put on a harness and dangle out over the stadium."

"Cool." Also hell no. I'm not a fan of heights. I'm just relieved it isn't a band venue. My luck has held so far with no one recognizing me, but if there are musicians in town, that luck will run out real fast.

"You'll like Fremantle," the driver says, turning off the highway and into the side streets of a town. "It still has all the Victorian-era architecture. Real pretty for tourists."

Luke nudges me, the slight pressure from his knuckle against my hip sending waves of pleasure through me. "Do you like sightseeing, Nora?"

"I don't know. It's been so long since I've gotten to go on a real vacation."

"The house is right on the beach," Luke explains. "Hopefully there's a nice view."

The driver eyes us in the rear view mirror. Eight years of performing have made me an expert at figuring out when I'm being watched. "How long have you two been together?"

My breath catches in my chest, but before I can eke out some lie, Luke loops his arm around my shoulders and kisses the top of my head. No chance I'll be able to breathe now. "Two years," Luke says to the driver, an easy smile on his face. "Trust me, I know how lucky I am."

A soft inner glow warms me and I snuggle closer to Luke. Daring myself, I run my hand over his chest, looping my fingers through the buttons to tease his hard flesh beneath the fabric. "You'll need to get changed, honey." My voice doesn't sound like me, it's almost a purr. Luke's gaze flashes to mine and there's a hit of heat there that even I can't miss. Apparently I needed a five-hour flight and the complete absence of my parents for my libido to wake up, but now it has and all sensors are tuned to Luke.

He covers my hand with his and pries it from his chest, kissing the back of my knuckles. "Will do."

Excitement shoots through me. The driver turns onto a wide street with cozy cottage-type houses on either side. Through the breaks between the walls of the homes, I can see the Indian Ocean in the near distance. I am on vacation. I am free. I am here with a man who has no idea that I am Honora Grand and he wants to be with me anyway. Well, I did pay him for that, but I can indulge in a little fantasy.

"Here we are." The driver stops in front of a little teal-colored bungalow with a white wraparound porch and a giant statue of a tortoise in the white-rock-covered front lawn. "Enjoy Perth. It's the best hidden gem in the world. Don't forget to get a toastie."

Luke slides out first, then holds out a hand to help me up. Lots of men have done this for me over the years, especially if I'm in a miniskirt and six-inch heels. But my palms have never sparked at anyone's touch before. I haven't flushed with the pleasure of being so attended. If I'm not careful, I'm going to lap at his heels like a cocker spaniel, and that is the least sexy thing I can imagine.

"What's a toastie?" I ask. The rain has stopped, but the air is cool and smells of salt.

"Sort of like the world's best grilled cheese, and don't tell Wisconsin I said that." Luke pecks me on the cheek and then takes out his phone, waving to the driver. "Five stars, mate. Cheers."

"Cheers." The driver waves a hand in the air, then takes off back toward the center of town.

I stand in front of the golden tortoise statue, my limbs numb with indecision. It's far easier to focus on the décor than on what will happen this week. Who on earth puts a massive tortoise in their front lawn? I like these people. "So."

Luke heads for the lockbox on the door and keys in a code. "So." The front door swings open on perfectly-oiled hinges.

"Wow." I rock back on my heels, trying not to stare too openly at Luke's very appealing ass as he walks into the house. "That was very little fanfare. I'd expected some champagne popping or a gong or something, since it's going to be the site of my debauchery."

Luke's laugh fills the small entryway with its simple, tan-colored jacket hooks and smooth brown floor. "Sorry it's not all silk and satin. It was the best I could do on short notice."

"It's perfect." I hesitate for a moment before coming up behind Luke and wrapping my arms around his waist. To his credit, he doesn't stiffen or pull away. He stands there, letting me set the pace. Leaning my cheek against his back, I press my chest against him and indulge in a good, long breath. "Thank you, Luke."

When he speaks, his voice shudders through his chest and into mine. "You could return that thanks by telling me more about yourself, you know."

Why oh why does he have to ruin it? I let myself have one more squeeze of perfect male and pull away. "I'm not that interesting. How do we do this?" I have to distract myself, distract him. I'm having so much fun just being Nora. I don't want that to change, not now, not before I've done what I came to do. The living room is just off the entryway, and set with bamboo furniture and driftwood sculptures. I perch on the edge of the couch and unzip my hoodie. "We can do it here. This couch is soft." I want him. This is not a surprise, or it shouldn't be, but it feels good. Sex is meant to be relaxing, and if I keep wondering how and when it's going to happen, I'll never fully unwind.

Luke doesn't move from his spot by the doorway. His hands slide into the pockets of his pants and his brow furrows. "Nora."

I know that tone. He's going to talk me out of this. He's going to tell me that I'm too nice, or this isn't the right time. "I know what I want." I take off my hoodie and I can't miss the brief flash of his gaze on my breasts through my tank top. It lingers a beat too long for him to be indifferent. I might as well make the best of it. I've spent years perfecting the art of looking sexy but unattainable. Well, Luke can attain me. I lean back against the couch, resting on my elbows. A photographer once told me that this pose made my breasts *look like the fucking Himalayas, gorgeous, darling.* He had no right to say it, but it's true, and I can use it to my advantage.

"I'm ready, Luke."

He stares at my face, his expression unreadable. "Nora, we have time."

"I'm tired of wasting time." I sound like a whiny toddler, but I don't care. This is the one thing on my to do list, then I can veg out for the rest of the week so I can have the headspace to figure out how to unfuck my life. "Please. Luke, I want you."

He crosses the room toward me, his steps slow and measured. Each inch closer is another shot of adrenaline that courses straight through my body and lands somewhere deep in my center. Kneeling before me, he cups my jaw between his palms. "Nora." His voice is soft, but somehow cuts through my skin and reverberates in my bones.

"I want to kiss you," I say. Memories of his kiss from last night are still imprinted on me, and it's all I can think about. "Please."

He brushes my lips gently with his, and even that soft caress is enough to send want flaring through me. But I can't move, because he has my face in his hands. It's dizzying, desiring him this much and not being able to move forward, to set the pace. "Nora," he says, his voice cutting through my brain fog. "We have time." He kisses my forehead, then releases me. "I need a shower. I imagine you wouldn't mind one either. The clothes and stuff I ordered should be here soon. I promise I will treat you the way you deserve, but let's prepare ourselves first, okay? I don't want your first time to be rushed."

Damn him for being logical. "I don't mind rushed."

Luke laughs softly and stands. "Well, I mind. It's a big responsibility to be your first, regardless of the importance you place on virginity. You deserve to be treated like a queen, Nora, and I can't do that smelling like airplane."

Ugh, I hate that he has a point. I hate that my clit has awoken and seems remarkably attuned to Luke's presence. It's like a damn homing beacon, and the closer he is, the hotter I get. But he isn't saying no, just not yet.

Maybe the anticipation will make it all sweeter. Or maybe he's messing with me.

"Do you trust me?" He holds out a hand to me and I examine it. Do I? I barely know him, but so far he's been nothing but kind, funny, and a gentleman, which is not exactly why I hired him. But if I think too hard on the fact that I'm just a job to him, and not really his fake girlfriend, that grates on my insides like Parmesan on a rasp. That moment in the car when he said we'd been together for two years? That felt way too good. My longest prior relationship was three months, which ended when he called my Purity

Pledge "a fucking Medieval chastity belt" and my parents "worse than Jim Jones." Of course I dumped him. They're not that bad. Quite.

That doesn't seem to be Luke, and even if he's hiding his flaws because he's very, very good at his job, I appreciate what he's done.

"Yes. Yes, I trust you."

CHAPTER 16

uke

THANK hell I had the sheer luck to book a cottage with two bedrooms and two showers. My dick is still punishing me after leaving Nora, but this is for the best. She deserves more than the bare minimum, and the bare minimum is not smelling like sweat and airplane fuel.

I step out of the shower and wrap a towel around my waist. Steam has fogged up the mirror, so I wipe it with a flat palm. I've looked at myself a lot over the years. Luke Bautista. The guy from Menomonee Falls whose dad left for work when I was nineteen and never came home. The guy who lies to his mom about what he does so she doesn't worry about him.

Okay, that last part is only half true. She knows I am a flight attendant, just not the other aspects of my chosen profession.

Oddly, thinking about my job irks me deep under my

skin, like someone has lined my muscles with the onion grass I used to find in my parents' backyard. It's bothered me a few times over the years. I got over it then and can get over it now. It's easier once I remember how this is all a fantasy. Nora's fantasy—or Honora's fantasy—depending on who we're talking about.

Though even in the short time I've known her, I know she is the same person. She contains multitudes. She's sunshine in a rainstorm and tastes like it, too. She's the light who is going to get me out of my predicament with Tobias and save my mom from her cheap ass medical insurance.

That's what I need to focus on. Not what my parents would think. I'm doing this for them.

I dab on a small amount of the aftershave that arrived with the rest of the supplies I ordered. Showtime.

I STEP out of the bedroom and freeze in place. Why the fuck didn't I put on pants? This towel does absolutely nothing to hide my rapidly growing erection.

Nora leans back against the couch, her blonde hair hanging in loose, damp waves around her face. She has gone for the Only Towel look as well, but it looks far, far better on her.

"Hello," she says, glancing down at my dick, peeking out from between the lines of the towel. I debate hiding, but fuck it. It's the reason we are here. "Did you have a nice shower?"

I can't move a single muscle in my body. Every cell calls out Nora's name. She smells of the shampoo and body wash provided by the house rental, and she looks like a walking wet dream. "Is this really what you want, Nora?"

She tilts her head, as if deciding. She knows what I'm asking. Hell, she's already asked enough. I should be man enough to listen to her when she speaks, to accept that she knows her own mind. It doesn't change how badly I need to hear those three little letters.

"Yes," she says simply.

I rush toward her, fold myself around her body and lift her to me. It isn't enough to kiss her, I want to taste her, explore her. My dick tells me just to bend her over and do what she's asked, but my head and my heart won't let me. No matter how good it feels when she slides her tongue into my mouth, taking as much as I'm giving. There isn't room in this embrace for oxygen. She folds her arms around my neck and pulls me closer to her. I wrap her legs around my waist and carry her toward the bedroom I just vacated.

"Luke," she whispers, her voice a plea of desperation.

I need to be in control, at least for a little while. I press her back on the bed and continue the kiss. She tastes like fresh minty toothpaste and I'm glad I had the presence of mind to brush before my shower. Moaning in a way that sends shivers all through my body, she glides her hand down my back to my waist, and the towel I'm wearing falls to the floor. A gust of wind rushes across my naked ass, which is just enough reminder that I had plans, and she's ruining them. In the best possible way, but still. This is her first time, and I will make it special if it fucking kills me.

And it might.

Summoning some form of inhuman strength, I break the kiss and prop myself above her. Damn my life, she's gorgeous. I tell her so, and her cheeks flush with desire and pleasure. The hem of the towel barely covers her bottom, and those long athletic legs speak naughty words to me.

"Do it now." Wrapped in her towel, Nora spreads her legs, bracketing me between her knees. "I'm ready."

Her conviction is both the hottest thing I've ever heard and another reminder that I should slow down. So what if my cock is dripping at the thought of being inside her?

My parents taught me to be a gentleman.

"I had plans, Nora. I'm not going to do it like this. Regardless of how you view virginity and sex, this is your first time. I don't want to hurt you. I can make it better. We're not teenagers in some rando's basement pool room." I stroke one finger down her cheek, her smile letting me know that she would rather do it this way, too. "You seem like the kind of person who, once she's made up her mind, will stop at nothing to accomplish that, and I respect it. But let's make this worthwhile."

Her knees fall inward, resting against the bare flesh of my hips, and that little bit of skin contact makes my own personal convictions that much more difficult to remember. "What did you have in mind?"

An excellent question, one whose answer seems very far away at this moment, because ninety-five percent of my body only sees Nearly Naked Nora.

Trailing a finger across her collarbone, I kiss a line along her chest, right above the line of the towel. "You've kissed someone before, right?"

"Yes."

"Have you been naked in front of someone before?" I have a feeling I know the answer. I've met other performers, and they have to be very comfortable with a quick change.

She shifts slightly beneath me. "Yes."

I bend and kiss the angle where her neck meets her shoulder, and she inhales quickly. "Stand up with me." Holding out my hand to her, I ignore the throbbing of my cock as I stand naked in front of her.

Her expression confused but intrigued, she takes my hand and stands in front of me, still wrapped in a towel. With my hands on her shoulders, I guide her until she faces the full-length mirror that makes up half of the closet door.

"What are you doing?" She turns her head to look at me,

and at that moment, I tug a little on the hem of her towel, and it falls to the floor. She gasps and makes a vain attempt to cover herself.

"If you want to be covered, that's fine." I nip at her earlobe, loving her little groan. "Or you could trust me."

She only hesitates for a moment before lowering her arms to her sides. I line myself up behind her, wrapping my arms around her waist. When my erection taps against her ass, she gasps again and then laughs.

"How do you feel?" I ask over her shoulder, meeting her gaze in the mirror.

Now that the initial surprise has left, she merely looks pleased and turned on. "I'm fine."

I stroke the sides of her stomach and trace the lines of her waist. "Has anyone ever touched you here?" I run a hand up to the underside of her small, perfect breasts. Her nipples pebble into little brown peaks at my touch.

She bites her lip as my fingers glide across her skin. "Not like this."

I want to murder every single asshole who ever thought he could take advantage of her. "Has anyone ever kissed them?"

In the mirror, her gaze meets mine, defiant and alive. If I'm not careful, I'm going to fall for this woman, and that will fuck my life even more than I've managed to do.

It would be a pretty spectacular fall.

"No," she says.

Failing to keep my cool, I indulge in a kiss at the base of her throat, where I can feel her pulse quicken beneath my lips. I cup her perfect breasts in my hands and then focus on her nipples, rolling them between my fingers and squeezing. She moans and leans into my touch. As if it knows exactly how full of shit I am, my cock throbs.

Down, boy. I'm sticking to my plan.

"Luke," Nora whispers, closing her eyes and leaning her head back against my shoulder as I lavish attention on her breasts. "That feels so good."

I stop and drop my hands to the arches of her hip bones. "Open your eyes. Tell me to stop if you aren't comfortable. Look at how beautiful you are."

She does, watching me with hunger in her gaze as I move from behind her to the front. From here, I can smell the sweet, tangy scent of her arousal. Yup, sunshine. I can taste her later.

I move to kneel in front of her.

Looking in the mirror, Nora gasps. "What happened to you?"

That sounds like a mood killer. I turn and see the massive bruise blooming across my flank. Thanks a fucking lot, Tobias. He spared my face but I hadn't quite thought to hide the other injuries. "I'm fine. Don't worry about it."

"Luke—"

I wrap my arms around her, feeling all the tension in her body. "It doesn't matter. You matter."

She relaxes in my embrace. "Tell me if it hurts."

"I like it when it hurts." The statement draws an arch smile. "Put your hands in my hair," I tell her, and when she does, lightning strikes of sensation curl from her fingers into my scalp. I curl toward her and take one of her sweet, plump nipples into my mouth. She barks, flexing her fingers as I lave the sensitive skin, pulling and tugging and sucking. This will get her mind off the bruise on my back.

"Fuck, Luke," she gasps, pulling me closer to her body, giving me more of herself.

"Is this all right?" I ask before switching to the other breast.

"Yes. Absolutely, yes."

So I don't stop. She begs me to continue as I fondle and

caress and suck and nip, her nipples hard and moist in my mouth. Every time I lick her and she cries my name, my cock throbs, begging for me to do what she is asking and sink into her body.

Not yet. She's not ready for me yet. Mentally, yes. But physically? If I don't want to hurt her, we still have more to do.

She arches her pelvis against my chest, seeking pressure.

"Do you want something, sunshine?" I ask, leaving her breasts for the time being and kissing a line down the center of her body.

"More." She keeps her eyes open, and I meet her gaze as I lick the skin around her belly button. "More. Please."

"Keep watching in the mirror." My gaze never leaves her as she watches our reflection. Her cheeks are flushed and her eyes bright and full of want. I cup her mound with one hand, then use one fingertip to run over her soft folds. She groans, rubbing against my hand. "Has anyone ever touched you here, sunshine? Has anyone ever tasted you?"

"No. No, I never wanted anyone to before." She bites her lip as my finger slips between her folds. "Not until you. I want you, Luke."

That hits deep, deeper than I expected. Plenty of women and men have said they wanted me, but no one has said it with some depth of emotion. Like I matter to them as more of a person than a body to perform a task. That is one of the issues with sex work. Sometimes it becomes routine. Today, with Nora? Anything but routine.

I part her folds, exposing her sex. "You are so gorgeous." I bend down and kiss her soft, private skin, and she moans, rocking against my face. "Can I touch you here?"

"Please. If you don't..." She laces her fingers in my hair again and tugs at the strands, causing just enough pain that it feels good.

So I do. I find her clit and take it in my mouth. Her response is immediate, clenching around me, her legs trembling. "Luke," she whispers.

I flick her clit with my tongue, and slide one finger along her seam. Her body shivers. "Yes." Her consent, her breath. I slide one finger into her tight opening, and she inhales sharply. "Yes," she repeats.

I worship her with my tongue and my finger, stroking her, spreading her, learning what makes her cry out and what makes her wetter.

As we find our rhythm, she grinds against me, pressing her beautiful pussy into my face, and I give her the friction and pressure she craves. My entire body sings out her name.

Nora.

"Luke—" she gasps. I never realized how much I missed having someone cry out my actual name.

She deserves a reward. As I suck hard on her clit, I slide a second finger into her. She sparks and cries out at the intrusion, but then she breaks, and her orgasm is the most spectacular thing I have ever been a part of.

CHAPTER 17

I ERUPT on his fingers and tongue in a way I had not known was possible. Who knew how sexy it is to watch an extraordinarily gorgeous man go down on you? My inner walls clench around him as I cry out his name, and I pull on his hair so hard it must hurt, but he doesn't stop holding me. He doesn't stop strumming that spot on my front wall that sends so much pleasure shooting through me, I feel electrocuted.

The spasms subside, and I release his hair as he licks the juice from my inner thighs.

"You are amazing, sunshine," he whispers, each stroke of his tongue a reminder of how well he just fucked me. My pussy clenches again, wanting him. Wanting more.

"Me?" I can't believe I can talk, but apparently I am capable of speech. "Luke, that was…I don't even have words."

But I do. Even now, in the fog of my post-orgasmic brain,

words flutter around, coalescing into lyrics and stanzas. I haven't written in ages, but maybe Luke has been the key.

My body's reaction to him is so intense. When we are together, I feel a little more whole, more seen.

After I've calmed down, he stands before me and wraps his arms around me, pulling me toward him in a hug. "How are you?" he asks softly.

Delirious. Thrilled. "I never want to leave this room." I hug him back, loving the way his skin feels against mine. He smells like the body wash and something else, something deeper, more Luke. Like cinnamon apple cider and fresh laundry.

His laugh reverberates through my chest. "We don't have to do anything else."

His erection presses against me, and a combination of happy hormones plus my earlier conviction reminds me that despite him giving me my first non-solo orgasm, I'm still, technically, a virgin. Not the plan.

So I spread my legs and rub my still-wet lips over his cock, loving the hardness of him against me and his shiver as he glides through my folds. "You promised, Luke."

He groans again as I slide over him another time. "You won't be stopped, will you, sunshine?"

"No." I wrap my arms around his neck and kiss him, loving how he tastes, loving how he feels. More than that, I love how I feel. Powerful. In command of my own sensuality. No one is sitting around with a camera, telling me how good I would look if I showed more skin. No Pastor Curt making offhand comments about how they used to test for virginity.

It's just Luke, who appreciates every non-airbrushed curve.

He lifts me up, changing the angle of our mouths so he kisses me more deeply, and it feels like that tongue is between my legs again. Luke. For the rest of my life, I will never forget Luke.

Turning, he sits on the edge of the bed and maneuvers to drop me beside him. "Give me a moment." His voice is calm but there's an edge of strain, like he's trying to hold back. He stands, giving me an ample view of his killer ass, and picks up a paper bag that was delivered earlier.

A sudden burst of anxiety runs through me. What am I doing? If I stare at his cock, is that weird? What is it going to feel like? Shit, what if it doesn't fit and I'm somehow deficient? What if it hurts? What if I bleed?

Why did I turn off everything on my phone after sending that quokka video so I can't even text Billie about all of this?

Luke takes out a packet of condoms and a small bottle of lubricant, but he stops when he sees my expression. He drops everything and kneels beside me on the bed. "Nora? Are you okay?"

"I—I don't know." I sound like I'm having a panic attack, which is appropriate because this definitely feels like a panic attack.

"Talk to me, sunshine."

I close my eyes, but the sound of a thousand sermons rattles around in my head. *Bad girl. Slut. Whore of Babylon.* But how can this be bad, when it feels so good, when it feels so right?

Luke tucks a still damp curl of hair behind my ear, drawing my attention back to him. "Where's your head, sunshine? Talk to me."

"I don't know. I'm all jumbled. All my life, my parents and the church and everything has told me that sex before marriage is wrong. We're meant to procreate."

"Women exist for men's pleasure?" He traces the outline of my ankle, but it helps.

"Exactly. Pastor Curt actually used to say that, the asshole."

"Pastor Curt?"

There's an undercurrent of danger in his tone that thrills through me. Luke is all sorts of wonderful. My protector, my hero.

"You don't need to slay any dragons for me." I shift so our bodies line up, and I can reach that bruised area on his back. "He made a lot of misogynistic comments to me, a few passes. One time…but my brother Dawson showed up and helped me. Probably the last time he helped me, honestly. I was able to fend him off, but it still feels greasy every time I think about him. It's why I stopped believing so blindly in the church." I've never said that aloud before, not even to Billie. "I'm okay."

With one arm around me, he's like a weighted blanket. "Don't minimize what that dickhead did to you. It was inappropriate. Of course you fought him off, because you're strong, but you never should have been in that position."

It's so unexpected and exactly what I think I've always needed to hear. Tears well up in my eyes and I do nothing to stop them. I can't believe I'm crying in front of this man, this practical stranger. But that's the thing about Luke. I might have known him for less than twenty-four hours, but I feel so comfortable with him. He doesn't want anything from me except my own pleasure.

Talk about hitting the jackpot.

He leans toward me and kisses the tip of my nose. "Think about me instead."

"Like I can think about anything else." I snuggle closer to him, as he wipes away the tears from my cheeks. "This isn't wrong, is it, Luke?"

"Sometimes when it's wrong, it's right. Or the wrongness makes it feel better." He laughs shallowly. "That made more sense in my head. What I mean is, sex is not inherently a bad thing. It's bad if there isn't consent or trust or if there's abuse. Even in married couples, people abuse one another for sex or power or, I don't know, fucking boredom. But between people who want the same thing, who seek pleasure or comfort, there's nothing wrong in that."

My own parents probably fall into the first category. I can't remember a time when my mom didn't cower in front of my dad, while still constantly doing anything to please him. Like pimp out her own daughter to the vagaries of the music industry. I've always known that it doesn't have to be that way. "Was it like that with your parents?" I ask.

He takes several moments to respond. "My parents adored each other. Even when they fought, I always knew they respected each other."

He moves his body so his knee slips between my legs, and pleasure zings through me. "Focusing so much on purity is a way to divide and control people. It isn't real, Nora. You're pure if you're true to yourself."

He's right, of course he is, and they were wrong. My family, Marvin, the church. They used my purity pledge to control me, but I need to be in charge of my own life. "Why does everything make sense when I'm with you?"

"I'm wicked smart and sexy," he responds. "It's the Midwesterner in me."

"Yes. You are all those things." I swing my leg over him and he rocks onto his back, holding me by my hips. I'm ready for this. I'm ready for him. "I want you, Luke."

He pulls me down toward him and kisses me until I can't determine where I end and he begins. Hands, lips, chest, legs. My nipples pebble as they rub against the light dusting of hair on his chest. Warmth and heat explode through me and I groan, pressing my wet pussy against his leg. Contact, I need contact and pressure.

His hands trail down my sides until one cups my ass and the other slips between my legs and finds the spot where I need it most. His steady thumb rubs my clit in tiny circles, gradually increasing the pressure, until I'm grinding against his hand. He's right. This isn't wrong. We are both consenting adults, and this pleasure is as close to godliness as I can imagine.

"Now," I say. "Do it now."

"Condom first." Aargh, why is he the best guy?

I lean over his side where he left the condom packet and hand it to him, but he also picks up the lube.

I've never watched anyone put on a condom before. I mean, obviously, but it's surprisingly appealing. His cock is surprisingly appealing. Not as long as the banana I've seen used in videos, but it's thick and dark and swollen, the rubbery crown leaking from a little slit at the top. Definitely better than Pastor Curt, that micro penis. I wonder what Luke tastes like. Maybe he'd let me try.

Luke's movements are so swift, so assured, as he sheathes his thick cock, then he squeezes out some of the lube. "You want to do this part, Nora?" His gaze is dark and full of wanton promises, and his voice has lowered two registers into make-my-undies-wet territory. "Have you done this before?"

I hesitate, but only for a second. "No. But I'm a fast learner." I kneel beside him. He takes my palm and swipes the lube onto it. It's warm from his hands.

"Rub it on me." He lies back, his erection sticking straight up to the sky.

I start at the tip, running my wet thumb across the rubber. Luke looses a deep groan, so I keep going. I squeeze lube over his entire cock, covering the entire sheath of condom. He's hot and hard in my hand, and I love how powerful I feel right now.

"This is your show, Nora." He puts his hands on my hips and lifts me until I'm straddling him. "Tell me what you want, what you're comfortable with."

Summoning all my deep inner resources, I slide over his slick length and notch his tip at my entrance. "You. I want you. All and everything." Spreading my legs wide and keeping my eyes closed, I exhale and sink down on his cock. The sensation is similar to his fingers. I'm grateful he stretched me first, and I'm soaking still from his mouth and my orgasm and the lube.

"Go slow, sunshine," Luke says.

So I do. I control my descent on his cock, stretching around him as I take him into my body, inch by inch. It's a little sore and completely new, but I'm so wet and aroused, I don't care. I feel like laughing and crying. Luke. Luke fills me up. As I try to drop lower, there's a sharp ache, but I'm ready for it. If I look at the connection between us, he isn't all the way inside me yet, and that's what I want. He's a little mini heater, deep in me, and even as it aches, I like it. No, love it. I exhale again and open wider, taking him in the last few inches.

A cry escapes me, but Luke catches it with a kiss. With a shift of his hips, he slides all the way up into me. It's pain and pleasure and fulfillment and I like it.

"Are you okay?" he asks.

"Yes. Yes, more."

He flips me onto my back and moves inside me, the motion bouncing my breasts. "Touch me," I whisper.

He leans down and captures my nipple between his lips, his teeth scraping the tip and I cry out again. I buck my hips against him, seeking the friction my body so desperately needs.

"Nora." Luke pulls out and then slides back into me, again

and again, each time hitting my clit and making pleasure spiral out through me. "You want to come, sunshine?"

"Yes." I watch where he thrusts into me, and I can't believe this is my life. I am so fucking lucky. "Yes, I want that."

He reaches between us and rubs my clit in tight, tiny circles and my pleasure climaxes. I cry out and arch into him, seeking him everywhere I can. Luke. I want to drown in Luke.

He lifts one of my legs over his shoulder as I'm still rolling through my orgasm, sliding into me again and again until I feel him buck and heat shoots through me. I want to watch him come. I force my eyes open. His are closed, his eyes shut tightly, the veins in his neck prominent. I did this to him. He did this to me.

And fuck yes, I want to do it again and again and again. Purity pledge be damned.

 ora

MY BRAIN FOGS and my entire body feels limp. I'm relaxed for the first time in I can't even remember how long, and I owe it all to him.

Luke Bautista.

He slides out of the bed and throws out the condom in the bathroom. I'm not sure what my favorite picture of him is. Walking away or coming toward me. Maybe on top of me. Definitely while he is on his knees...

I yawn and stretch my limbs. Naked, Luke comes back, tucking me in and handing me a glass of water and an ice pack. I want to wrap my arms around him, rest on his chest, burn the memory of him into me. But a twinge of anxiety keeps me still.

"So, what's the protocol?" I ask.

He yawns and turns to me. "Protocol for what?" He has a patch of dark hair smattered across his chest.

"I don't know." I play with the sheets covering my chest. I'm never naked at home, not unless I'm showering or changing. It's different, luxurious to feel the linens against my skin. I don't know why I'm having such difficulty talking to him. "Snuggling, maybe."

He opens his arms wide and pulls me toward him until I'm happily snugged against his side, breathing in the post-coital scent of sex and his sweet sweat. "Snuggle away, sunshine."

Unsurprisingly, he is the world's best big spoon.

We lie there in bed. I think he's dozing, because his breathing is so even, but my thoughts won't slow down enough for sleep. "So…rando's basement pool table?" I ask.

Luke laughs. "Yup."

I run my hand over his chest, liking the way the soft short hairs bristle under my palm. "Is that how you lost your virginity?"

He sighs a little but his arm tightens around me, like he's happy to be here. With me, plain mysterious Nora. Would it be different if he knew I was Honora Grand? "Yeah. Mackenzie Lovette. Senior year." He tucks a curl of hair behind my ear. "I thought I was such a stud, and I only lasted like five minutes."

"Senior year of high school?" I didn't go to my senior year. By that point, I had GED tutors. I always wanted to go to a prom or homecoming dance, or even just go to some ridiculous teenage party. I've missed too many rites of passage, but hearing about Luke's makes me feel better.

"Yeah."

"How was it?"

He tilts his head and laughs. "I was disappointed in myself. My mom loves romance novels, like, *loves* them. She reads all the time, and leaves them around the house. I started picking them up when I was about fourteen, so maybe I had a skewed view of how sex works. Mackenzie definitely wasn't a 'fountain' and most women actually don't orgasm with penetration. You are a beautiful exception."

I've heard this before, too, but I like that he's talking so frankly about it. It's a refreshing change from the fingers-in-the-ears-la-la-la my own parents do. "Did you get better in college?"

"I hope so. I was more of a one-girl-guy in college."

Oof. This stings. I wonder who she is and why I suddenly don't like her. "Did you break up after graduation?" Is he single? I mean, I thought this whole thing was consensual, but I don't want to be that woman. Questions I should have known to ask.

"I didn't graduate from college."

My ears prick up, even as a tinge of realizing he didn't actually answer the question. "Really? Why not?"

He shrugs and turns his head away from me. "I did a study abroad trip junior year, fell into the, um, life. It was good money, I enjoyed it, so I never went back to school."

"Oh." I forget sometimes that he's only here because this is a job. He makes it so real, it's difficult to remember he isn't my actual boyfriend. "I never went to college, either."

"Why not?" It's nice to have a question someone doesn't assume they already know the answer to.

"I wanted to." I kiss the top of his sternum, just because I can, and I want to soak in every moment possible. "I wanted to study marine biology or maybe child psychology. But my parents refused to let me apply."

"That sucks."

Yes, it does, and now they want me to marry some stranger. Well, fuck them. I have a petty urge to text them that I'm currently in bed with a gorgeous sex worker. That will make my mom clutch her crucifix.

"Your parents don't make you do anything?" I snuggle

closer. He's so warm, I wonder if I'll be cold the minute he's gone.

"It's just me and my mom. She's still in Wisconsin."

"What happened to your dad?"

Beneath my hand, I feel his breath hitch in his chest. "He—he died when I was nineteen." He says it like it's not something he's fully admitted, even to himself.

"Luke, that's awful."

"Yeah, yeah it was. But we're okay. For the most part." There's more he isn't saying, more to this story, and I want to know everything. Not from some deep gossipy urge, but because I care about him. So what if this isn't real, if it's only one week? He's so many things, this kaleidoscope of a man. Certainly the most interesting one I've ever met.

I lean my cheek against his chest and close my eyes, sleep closing in fast. "You can tell me. If you want. I'd like to know anything at all."

He pauses then kisses the top of my head. "Thanks, sunshine."

"Thank you for today."

As I drift to sleep, he pulls me so close I'm completely lining his body, and it feels like he is the puzzle I've been missing from for my whole life.

"Anything for you," he whispers as I drift off to sleep.

CHAPTER 19

uke

I WAKE up wrapped in Nora, the dim sunlight of morning streaming across the bed. I'm starving and I have massive morning wood from her proximity. Which does not lessen when she stretches against me, her puckered nipples scraping across my chest, the damp folds of her pussy warm against my leg.

Part of me wants to wake her up and see if she would be up for a repeat of last night. I've had a lot of sex, but last night felt different. Special. Maybe because we're here and I'm not actively being chased by Tobias and his goon squad, maybe because it was Nora's first time. I don't know. She might be famous, but there's a large part of me that thinks I will always remember this week, this woman.

Which brings up a whole other realm of thought, one that does finally ease the pressure in my throbbing cock. I might need to quit my job. I love Leather and Lace, I love making people feel good, but the endless parade, all of whom want me for "my special talents" and not really for me, is starting to wear. Maybe it's the romance novels of my teenage years, but I'm ready to wake up with the same person day after day. Fight with them, fuck them, laugh with them. Someone I can introduce to my mom.

Like that went so great last time.

Nora shifts, sliding her hand across my chest, and banishing all thoughts of girlfriends past. Her touch is fire and lightning and I love it. "Good morning." She kisses the top of my right pectoral, where she's been curled up all night. My right arm is a little numb, but it will get the feeling back. It's worth it, to wake up with her like this.

"Morning." Fuck me, she's beautiful in this pre-awake stage. Her eyes flutter softly, her eyelashes fluttering feathery kisses against my skin. "How are you feeling?"

Stretching in a cat-like way, her mouth pulls into a grin. "Amazing. A little sore, but amazing." As if to prove her point, she glides her leg over mine, letting me feel her warmth and heat.

Yup, morning wood has returned full steam.

She moves over me, her body brushing against mine, and every centimeter of her lights a massive fire inside of me. Kissing my neck, she lines up her pussy over my rock hard cock and strokes me twice. I can do nothing but groan and feel the sensation of her hot, wet silk over my erection. Thank fuck I'm not seventeen in a basement with Mackenzie Lovette any longer, or I would be unable to control my own release.

She leans over me to whisper in my ear, her hair falling over my face and chest in a curtain that I would happily wrap myself in. "I dreamed all night about you inside of me."

Okay. I'm awake now.

Grinning, but keeping my mouth away from hers because

morning breath is the worst, I flip her onto her back and go straight for her nipples. They're already hard and sensitive. The moment I take one in my mouth and suck on it, she laces her hands through my hair and arches into me. I roll her nipple on my tongue, savoring it, suckling it in tight little pulses.

I could definitely do this for the rest of my life.

"Luke," she whimpers, wrapping her legs around my waist. "I want you inside of me. Now."

"Done, sunshine." I kiss the side of her shoulder then extricate myself and find the package of condoms and the lubricant on the bedside table.

She rolls onto her side and watches as I roll on the condom. "Do we…do we really need that?"

"What?" I take a dollop of lubricant and stroke myself, starting at the base and running toward the head. She licks her lips, which makes me groan.

"The condoms. I mean, you know I haven't been with anyone else. I assume you get tested?"

"Yeah." I join her back on the bed and she curls into me, like I'm a magnetic pole she can't keep herself from. I fucking love it. "Spread your legs for me." She complies, and I take another dollop of lubricant and slide it between the lips of her pussy. She moans, rocking into my hand, so I let her have what she wants and circle her clit in small, tight movements. She warms beneath me. My cock throbs so badly it's difficult to think, but her question still gnaws at me. "What about pregnancy though? Honestly, I've never had sex without a condom."

"Oh." It isn't a question, more of a moan as she arches into my touch. I slide one finger into her, stretching her. "I—oh fuck, that feels so good—I have an IUD. I used to have really awful periods, and I couldn't perform, so my parents—oh, Luke!" I slide another finger into her wet, tight heat and she bucks against me. "Now. Please. I want to feel you move inside me now."

"Whatever you want." I prop myself above her and notch myself at her entrance. I plan on going slow, like last night, easing myself into her, but she reaches between us and takes my dick in her warm hand, and the tip glides in. "You are so perfect, Nora," I groan.

"More." She arches her back, spreading her legs wide and rocking her pelvis up, and suddenly I am balls deep in her and it is pure fucking heaven. "Yes. Yes, like that." Her breath comes in short, sharp pants as I move, fucking her slowly and sweetly. "Harder."

"I don't want to hurt you."

She shifts beneath me, seeking her own pleasure by adjusting our angle. "I can take it. Please."

Far be it from me not to listen to her. I take her ankles and throw them over my shoulder so I can drive into her, the way she begs me to. Each pulse against her sends a thousand signals of pleasure and desire through my brain, and each thrust resonates in my ears. *Nora.*

She holds onto me, digging her nails into my back, and the pain keeps me going even as she cries my name. I move a little so I can free one hand to circle her clit, and then she breaks, spasming around my cock as I drive into her, and the tight hot velvet of her around me is too much. With a final thrust, I release into the condom and collapse onto my elbows, propped above her.

Nora. Nora.

ora

HE GETS me an ice pack for the soreness and a large glass of water, then tucks me into bed with far too many pillows while he goes to make breakfast.

I wrap myself in the covers and watch him through the open door. He hums to himself as he walks around the kitchen in his boxers, the rest of his glorious body on display. What would he do if he knew he had fucked Honora Grand, Purity Princess?

Ugh, I'm not ruining this by thinking about that.

Though I do wish I could call Billie and squee, but I can't do that, either. She can't know where I am, for her protection as well as mine.

"Do you like peppers in your eggs?" Luke calls.

"Sure." My mother is always telling me to eat more vegetables. Egg whites only, Honora. No carbs, Honora. Well, Mom, fuck your restriction diet. "Is there toast?"

"Absolutely."

I hear the unmistakable dunking of bread into a toaster and my mouth waters.

"How do you take your coffee?" Luke leans against the doorway, and I can smell the roasted beans. "This place has an espresso machine. I learned how to make a flat white one slamming weekend in Mallorca, if you're interested."

"Sure." I have no idea what that is, but I trust him after that oat milk latte. I usually take it black per my nutritionist's orders, but that makes me hate the taste and so I only drink it in emergencies. The sugary, creamy drinks he's been making are nowhere near that stuff. "That sounds great."

"Cool." His smile is almost hesitant, but happy, light. Like he likes being here with me.

My vagina might be a bit sore now after our activities, but I can still feel the tingly warmth of him in my arms, inside my body. I'm happy being here with him, too.

WE SPEND the day on the deserted beach outside the house. The Indian Ocean is frigid this time of year, but the long stretch of white sand feels like heaven. Malibu isn't like this.

Luke makes me a toastie with ham and pickles, and it is hands down the best damned grilled cheese I have ever eaten. We find an old deck of Uno cards in one of the bookcases and play on the Fremantle beach.

"We should see Perth." He plays a wild card and draw four. "Sorry, sunshine. Oh, and blue."

Grr, I only have green and red, but I have to pick up four cards anyway. "I don't know. I don't really like going out much."

Understatement. Hiding out here with Luke is great, but what if we go out and someone spots me? There goes my happy little anonymous sex cocoon. Before, when I would sneak out, I'd use my cosmetics application skills to disguise my features. While we ordered some clothes and toiletries and groceries for the week, I don't exactly have putty for a false nose. If only I had thought to bring a full makeup kit when I stormed away from the stadium in Sydney.

I draw a blue seven and play it, and he puts down a six on his turn. "My friend told me about this place. I'd really like to take you. I think you'd enjoy it. It's not far from here, and we can go after dark."

My hand stills on the draw pile. He doesn't know who I am, does he? Maybe I should just tell him and get it over with. Then he'd understand why I don't date, why I don't go out in public unless I'm completely covered.

"Luke—"

He covers my hand with his. "Don't worry. No one will recognize you if you don't want them to. It's just some fun."

Fun. This is fun. Luke is fun. If I don't do this, what does that mean? Will he be mad at me? No, he doesn't seem that type, not even slightly.

When I look into his gaze, the only thing I see is warmth and kindness. "Okay."

"Okay." Luke grins. "Also, I can see your cards. Uno."

uke

SHE DRESSES IN HER HOODIE, leggings and pink sneakers again, covering the top half of her face with sunglasses, and I give her one of the KN95 masks I still always carry with me. Hey, my mom is immune suppressed. I gotta show support. "You okay?" I ask.

She looks at herself in the mirror, her lovely face covered and barely recognizable. Yes, I caved, and went down an Honora Grand internet rabbit hole, but all I see before me is Nora. Messy bun and red lipstick behind the black fabric of the mask.

"I'm okay."

We take a ride share into Perth's city center, but she still looks nervous. "I can't believe I beat you at Uno." I nudge her side with my hip.

"I let you win at Uno, you mean," she says.

I tickle her side and she devolves into a ball of giggles against the window of the car.

"You two are adorable," the driver says from the front of the car. "How long have you been together?"

"Six months," I say automatically, looping my arm through Nora's. "Don't tell her, but I'm going to marry this one."

I feel Nora's entire body flush under my hand. If I'm being entirely honest, she's not the only one. I've given flippant replies to that question with loads of people, but this time, it all feels different. Like in a parallel universe, if I were not a sex worker and Nora weren't a pop superstar whose family was in a Christian Mafia, maybe we really could be together. Maybe we could get married.

I can't deal in if onlys. Pay off Tobias, help Mom, be someone worthy of my dad's memory. Day dreaming about a life with Nora isn't on the checklist.

My heart churns in my chest like a bad case of acid reflux.

"Ah, you should. I've been married four times." The driver pulls into a car park near the Swan River. "Best thing for you, mate."

"Cheers." I pay him through the app on my phone and help Nora out. Outside of this cab, I have more control of the situation.

Or so I lie to myself.

She doesn't let go of my hand as I lead her through the streets of the city toward the club, and her presence distracts me from our surroundings.

Sure, Perth is gorgeous. Tree-lined streets, a mixture of brick and glass buildings. Looping art reminiscent of the waterways. I've never been here before, but I wouldn't mind spending more time. In some nebulous future once this week is over.

Yeah, there's that acidic burn in my chest again.

"You shouldn't joke about it," Nora says as we wait to cross an intersection.

"Joke about what?" Joking is my default, after all, but she sounds disturbed, which was not my intention for this evening.

"About us being together. We're not." As if to reinforce it, she pulls her hand out of my grasp. I stumble a little. "It's only a week."

Oh. Right. I conveniently forgot that we have an automatic expiration date. I don't really want to think about that at the moment. Maybe I should give her the money back.

Nope, definitely can't think about that. I have a persistent ache in my kidney to remind me why I can't return my auction fee.

Tobias. I can focus on that. One week and I can get rid of Tobias, as long as I keep Nora happy.

"Look." I stop her in the middle of the street under a massive colorful mural. If we can get through this part of the date, I want to take her on one of the art walks around Perth. "I know this is an odd situation, and I know you're uncomfortable being out." She shifts side to side, not looking at me. "I promise, I'll order you some hair dye before we go out again. But you said you'd never had a real date, and I want to take you on one. I might not really be your boyfriend—" weird, there's that uncomfortable itch at the back of my skull —"but the memories are real."

I can't see anything going on in her mind as her face is pretty well covered, but she's turned toward the mural. "Do you trust me, Nora?"

A few agonizing seconds pass before she tilts her head back to me and nods. "I trust you."

. . .

THE MOMENT we enter the club, Nora grips my arm tightly and squeals behind her mask. Her reaction lights me up inside.

"Seriously?" she asks, her head turning to take it all in.

It's a coffee shop and bar, with lots of small circular tables set in front of the stage and a few booths lining the back wall. Behind the bar there's an old-fashioned fogged glass mirror and a bartender with full tattoo sleeves. There's the stage, with a drum set and a microphone on a stand and a sign reading *Open Mic Tonight.*

"Do you want to sit down?" I point to one of the booths in the back. There are a lot of open seats, but I thought it would be better to get here before the crowds, to minimize Nora's chances of being recognized.

I kind of wish she would just tell me her big secret already so I can stop pretending I don't know. But this is her week. She shared a big moment in her life with me, and I shouldn't want more.

Nora pulls me by my hand to the booth, weaving her way through the unoccupied tables. There are only a few other patrons here tonight, a young person with a guitar at their side, an older white man with a beard that would put a lumberjack to shame, and a table of three women in jeans and denim shirts nursing three very large beers.

Seems pretty typical for an open mic night, in my opinion. It would blow all of their minds if they knew Honora Grand was sliding into this slightly sticky faux-leather banquette.

The bartender comes over to our table, holding a book in one hand. He's good-looking, his tattoos dark against his light brown skin and his trimmed beard very well maintained. "What can I getcha?" he asks.

"A pint," Nora says automatically. She plays with the cuffs of her sweatshirt, like she can't contain her excitement.

"Same."

The bartender doesn't write it down, but nods toward Nora's disguise. "Cool shades. You don't need a mask here if you don't want. We're all vaxxed."

"Thanks." Tentative, she pulls down the KN95, exposing those gorgeous red lips. Under the table, my cock swells at the thought of wrapping that pretty mouth around me, imprinting her lipstick on my dick.

I adjust myself as subtly as I can manage and try to think of other things.

Like how I loathe this bartender, who is looking Nora over like she's an iced mocha and he's been traveling the Outback for days.

Casually, I wrap my arm around Nora's shoulders. She's mine, Tattoo Dude. Back off.

The bartender tilts his head, but turns back, hopefully to get our beers and not poison me so he can steal my girlfriend. Fake girlfriend. Whatever.

"This place is amazing." Nora turns toward me, her smile so big it almost makes her petite face look larger. "How did you find it?"

My arm around her feels astonishingly normal and good, so I pull her a little closer to me "The magic of the internet. I thought you might like it."

"Love it."

The bartender returns with our beers and leaves them without comment, but I catch the way his gaze lingers a beat too long on Nora.

Normally I'm all for sharing, but not tonight.

I'm saved from my own inane machismo by the trio of women, who step up to the stage.

"All right to start then, Chris?" The youngest says. She has long blonde curls, nearly to her waist.

The bartender nods.

Only one of the trio brought an instrument, a fiddle. The other sits behind the drum set and the youngest steps up to the microphone. "We're the Opies of Osborne Park Hospital, in the neonatal nursing unit. Thanks for listening. This gets us through our shifts."

They play a folk cover of "Take on Me," which is rousing and heartfelt and surprisingly on tune. The woman playing the drums keeps the beat well and the singer has a nice soprano, but it's the way the three of them gel that's the most appealing.

Nora applauds loudly, cheering and whooping when they finish, as do the rest of the bar patrons.

The evening passes like this. We sip our beers and watch the other acts. A few others have come in now, and the person with the guitar seems reluctant to get up and sing. Nora settles into the booth, leaning her arms on the table, entranced. It's more fun in a lot of ways to watch her than the performances.

"So you performed in a place like this?" My beer isn't too hoppy, a nice even Aussie lager. Still, I can't have more than one without having dinner.

"Yeah." She's shed some of her nerves as it seems like no one here recognizes her. The bartender certainly doesn't seem like he would be a huge Honora Grand fan, though that might be my own perspective coloring the situation. "I used to love singing at open mics."

"Is that something you want to do? Sing?" I'm treading a fine line here, and I know it, but this would be the perfect opening for her to tell me. It feels like a secret we shouldn't be keeping from one another.

If I think about it, this is a professional arrangement and she's entitled to keep secrets, but I have a strange urge to tell her all of mine.

"I love to sing. I love music and how it makes people feel. That's all I ever wanted, to make people feel something, to make people remember me." She barks one sharp laugh. "That's not true. I wanted my parents to notice me but I think I knew even when I was young that it would never happen." Nora claps as the person with the guitar steps onto the stage. They're wearing navy blue board shorts and a gray long-sleeved T-shirt.

"Hello," they say. "I'm Whizz. I hope you like this song."

I'm still stuck on Nora's words. What is she talking about? I saw a few articles about her parents and her manager, who apparently run her life, but all the articles refer to what a close family they are.

Who am I to judge? No one ever knows what goes on behind a closed door, and you don't need to be a sex worker to know that.

The person starts playing their guitar, their sure fingers gliding through the chords of a song I haven't heard before but it's lovely. It's soft, folksy, about a light in the darkness. No, a lighthouse. It's the kind of song I want to hear if I'm having a bad day and need to unpack.

It reminds me a bit of the first Honora Grand song I ever really liked, one of her early ones. She—or her producers— remixed "Snake Skin" last year with a guest rapper, but I prefer the original version.

I watch Nora watching the performer. She's entranced, fully invested in the performance. A tear slips down the line of her nose. She's like my lighthouse. When I had nowhere to go, she guided me to safety. But she doesn't hold it over me or use it against me. She treats me like her equal, as if I could ever measure up to an international pop star who cheats at Uno. My lighthouse, my sunshine.

I know she isn't really mine.

She gives the performer a standing ovation when they finish, making them blush fiercely and bow several times. When she goes to talk to them, to congratulate them, it's like I can already feel her slipping through my fingers, and it feels like shit.

ora

BEST. Night. Ever.

I head back to our booth after congratulating Whizz and telling them how wonderful their song is. I bought their self-produced album. I'll never play it for Marvin, but Billie has a friend who is a manager, Louise Fields, and she would love it. "Wasn't that incredible?" I slide in beside Luke and hug him tightly. "I have this friend, well, Billie's friend and she—" Luke is not paying attention. His smile is forced and his shoulders are set. "What's wrong?"

He takes a large drink of his beer. "Nothing. Nothing's wrong. You're amazing, Nora. I hope you're having fun."

"I'm having the best time." I kiss his cheek, letting my lips linger there. "You are the best." It doesn't seem like the compliment is sinking in. An idea sparks in my brain and I grin widely. I'm still wearing my sunglasses. Maybe no one will notice me, and it's something I can do to make Luke smile.

I'd do pretty much anything to make Luke smile.

Some people are worth the risk. "Wait here." I kiss Luke one more time, this one on the lips, savoring the beer on his tongue, then head down to the bar. It's only five minutes of sweet talking—thank God there aren't that many people here —and a quick chat with Whizz, and then I'm heading toward the stage with a guitar.

I settle behind the microphone and strum Whizz's guitar. This is a beautiful, well-cared-for instrument. Go, Whizz.

How long has it been since I did this? Sang in front of fifteen strangers, none of whom expect anything of me?

It's past damn time.

"Hello everyone." My voice sounds smokier in the bar than it does piped through loudspeakers and amps during my stadium tour. I sound more like me. "This is for the best man I've ever met. Luke Bautista, the boy with dreams in his eyes."

Luke's gaze snaps to mine, full of surprise and heat.

I launch into my favorite remix of "Sunglasses at Night." It's a bit more stalker-y and angsty than I remember, but I don't care. It feels good to sing in this tiny bar in front of these kind strangers in this place that smells a bit like frayed electrical wires and stale booze. I sing it for Luke. He may have the deepest brown eyes I've ever seen, but he sees so much. I want to see the world through the colorful kaleido-scope of his gaze.

How could I have forgotten what it's like to perform in this intimate setting? Even though it's the smallest crowd I've sung in front of for years, every eye is on me like they actu-ally see me. Nora. Not the Honora Grand persona, the Silver and Gold Goddess, look but don't touch. Just Nora. Messy and wearing my old gray leggings and singing my heart out to a man I will never forget. No one here takes out their phone to record me. There are no pyrotechnics or complicated dance breaks or "surprise" cameo guests. No one cheers "Honora!" At the end of my song, I take a bow to the enthusiastic applause, hand the guitar back to Whizz with my undying thanks, and simply head back to my table to finish my beer.

It is the perfect night.

uke

"ARE you going to tell me where we're going?" she asks from the passenger seat of the pickup truck I rented. That's the thing I love about the current era. Anything can be delivered any time, just with the swipe of an app.

"Isn't the fun not knowing?" I follow the maps app on my phone, directing us away from our little bungalow in Fremantle, past Perth, then north toward the desert.

She settles into her seat, her face pressed against the window as the landscape unfolds around us. "You are full of surprises."

"Hey, I'm a full service station." It's bitter, I know, but my phone has at least twenty-four missed notifications from Tobias. Where am I? Where is the rest of his money? Do I know what a piece of shit I am?

It's like he doesn't believe me that the money is coming later this week, when Asta moves the bulk of it into my account. Fuck him. Mom needed the money first. Mom hasn't noticed yet that the creditors have stopped calling, but she will. I'll figure out something to say, eventually.

For all I pride myself on my ability to read people, to love them and leave them, this week with Nora has left me speechless.

Last night with Nora was incredible. I've heard her songs on the radio, but that live acoustic version of her, raw and hungry and full of emotion? She basically fucked my soul with that song, slow and deep. That ridiculous, angsty, early 80s Corey Hart song. It did something to me, something beyond that insistent voice at the back of my head that keeps whispering, *Mine.*

But she isn't. This is temporary. If those text messages are any reminder, I have a job to do and I cannot, absolutely cannot fuck it up by falling for the client. That's the oldest, most foolish mistake in the world.

And I'm not falling for her. Absolutely not. So what if her scent drives me up a fucking wall? So what if she and I spent the day in bed, dissecting Gerard Butler action movies and laughing our asses off? So what if I know how she likes her eggs in the morning, and, miracle of miracles, she knows how I like mine? She cooked breakfast for me today. Seriously. She burned it, but she tried. So what if no one has ever made me breakfast? Not even Mackenzie Lovette.

This is not real. I've been at this job way too long to believe in a magic pussy.

"This is really fun. I like getting out." Nora hugs her arms around herself, and something about the small gesture of pleasure sends a rush of adrenaline down my spine.

Yup. I am a professional.

. . .

THE SUN IS SETTING as we drive into Pinnacles National Park. Even during the drive up here, we could see the rocky karsts stretching to the sky from the desert floor. The gods have painted the sky in a rainbow kaleidoscope.

"This is amazing," Nora says, exhaling long and low.

"Seriously." The setting sun does something to the landscape, stroking it like the ground has been waiting all day to look this beautiful.

I pull into a parking space. "Come on."

She pushes open her door eagerly and hops down from the cab. She dressed today in her leggings and a loose-fitting exercise tank I bought her, and I have never seen anyone more beautiful, especially limned in the light of the desert sun, crimson and gold and mauve. "What is this place?" she asks.

"It's called The Pinnacles." She rolls her eyes, because she saw the sign leading her just as well as I did. "They're limestone formations, formed by the receding seas tens of thousands of years ago, leaving behind towers of seashells. Over the years, the wind erased the sand between the towers, and here we are."

"You're such a geology nerd."

"You say that like you're impressed, so I'll take it as a win."

She bumps my hip with hers, the small familiarity sparking something deep and warm inside me. Like getting out of school early to go sledding on the first snow day of the year.

Instead of wrapping my arms around her and kissing her until we both forget why we have come, I open the bed of the pickup and start arranging all of the supplies I packed. Blankets, food, water bottles.

"I've never been camping," Nora says, unrolling blankets in the truck bed. "Wait, that's not true. My dad took us once when I was eight. My mom *hated* it. We came home and she says it took a week and a half to get rid of the smell of campfire and mosquito repellant."

I climb into the truck bed beside her and pull her toward me. "We're in the middle of the desert, and I know absolutely nothing about the biology here, but I doubt there are mosquitos."

She shrugs and curls up on top of the blankets, leaning back against the window to the cab. "I didn't mind it at all. Not then and not now. I like being outside."

"Wine? Hot cocoa?" I hold out both containers to her and she chooses the hot cocoa. "I brought marshmallows, too."

"You are quite the barista."

The compliment warms me. "Thanks. It was one of my favorite odd jobs."

"What did you like best about it?"

I don't even need to think. "I made people happy."

"You make people happy now, just in a different way."

"That's certainly true." I make others happy. I pour myself a hot cocoa and add in three marshmallows. "My dad's family worked on a coffee plantation in the Philippines. So I've always been, I don't know, drawn to coffee."

Shit. I hadn't meant to say that. I stare up at the sky, filling with stars as the sunlight ebbs. I don't talk about my dad. Not since everything that happened after the funeral. Did I kill the mood? I glance at her.

Nora's gaze on me is warm and thoughtful. "Do you want to talk about your dad?"

Do I? "I don't know." I turn my attention back to the sky in this alien desert-scape. "I'm not sure why I said anything. You don't need to know that."

She slips her hand into mine and squeezes. "I like knowing."

A moment passes where it feels like every emotion I've

ever felt and buried is going to explode out of my chest like a mutant in a horror movie.

As if sensing my displeasure, Nora squeezes my hand again. "What would you do, if you didn't do what you're doing now?"

Night falls quickly around us now, the temperature dropping with it. In lieu of answering her very appropriate question, I pick up one of the thick blankets and wrap it around her shoulders. She kisses the bottom of my chin, bringing with her the scent of chocolate.

"I like your five o'clock shadow." She runs her fingertips over my jaw, rustling the bristles. "You didn't answer my question."

"I don't know." It's easier to talk about than my complicated feelings about my dad. I settle in beside her, pulling a blanket over my legs and staring up at the sky. There are a few clouds, but the inky black night is dotted with stars and a half-moon. "Really, I don't. I probably should have figured this out by now. I'm two years shy of thirty. But things have been working out, so I just haven't pushed it." I sigh as clouds pass over the moon. "I need to get on that. I can't really be a sex worker my whole life."

"Why not?" Nora sips her cocoa. "If you like it, why not keep doing it?"

Four million dollar question. "Can't you ask me what the constellations are?" I point above us. "I googled some this morning. That one is either the Jewel Box or a drunken moose."

She laughs, her shoulder reverberating against mine. "That's not a moose. It's an elk. Shouldn't a Wisconsin kid know the difference?"

"Ah, but you assume I was an outdoorsy Wisconsin kid, when in fact I was a giant nerd hiding out at my friends' houses from my very affectionate and loving parents."

One of her eyebrows ticks upward. "Hiding in basement pool rooms?"

"Touché."

She rests her head on my shoulder and stares upward at the sky. "Mackenzie Lovette doesn't know what she missed."

A cold spike stabs me in the heart. "She did, actually. She was my college girlfriend. We were together for four years."

"Really?" She doesn't look at me, but presses her body against mine.

"Yeah." I swallow. Since when am I Opening Up Guy? Normally I'm Deflect With a Joke Guy. Must be the hot cocoa.

"What happened?"

Flippant replies stall in my throat. I haven't talked about this, not in years, and only once with my mom. I hide in temporary relationships, nights of passion without the promise of love, because I can't get hurt like that again. I can handle a lot, but not that kind of pain.

It's Nora asking. Patient and waiting. Even if this is just one week in the span of our lives, I want her to know. I want someone to know me, to know what I've been through. "After, um, after my dad died, I was a mess. I took a month off from school to help my mom organize everything at home. Mackenzie couldn't deal. She said I was distant, that I wouldn't talk to her, that I was shutting her out. Then I found out she was secretly dating someone else, and had been since before my dad died."

"Ugh, what a bitch." Her reply is so automatic that it makes me laugh. She blushes softly. "Sorry."

"Don't be. I probably did push her away. At the time, it's what I thought I should do, but I don't know." The blanket falls from her shoulders, and I readjust it to keep the chill from her. That whole time is still such a blur. My mom needed so much, and I knew my dad would have wanted me there by her side. Mackenzie never saw it that way, but how could she when she had already been cheating on me?

"You're a good man, Luke. You were grieving and needed space and time. But maybe she wasn't the right woman for you."

As if my body knows something my brain doesn't, my arm squeezes her tight. "Maybe. What about you? What would you do if you weren't doing what you do?"

"Oof, I have no idea." Gazing at the sky, she traces the lines of the stars with her fingertips, like she's painting the images into her mind. "I don't think my family ever gives me the space even to contemplate something else." This does jibe with the little she has told me. It's almost cult-like, the way they overwork her, but I'm not supposed to know she's Honora Grand.

I really wish she would just tell me already.

"What do you like doing?" She's so close I can drop a kiss on the top of her soft hair. I can't decide how I like it best, up in a cute floppy bun or hanging around her shoulders as she's riding me. Definitely the second one.

"I want to get back to the songs I like to write and sing. Sometimes I get tired of other people's opinions." Her voice is quiet and her fingertip has stalled on the brightest star in the sky. Alpha Centauri? An airplane? I have zero idea but I like being here, doing this, with her.

A long moment passes while I debate telling her that I know who she is, and that I could honestly give two flying fucks. I like her any way she chooses to be. "You should. Your voice…it's otherworldly. You should do what you love."

The clouds above us shift as the night darkens, and the Milky Way is on full, glorious display. It's otherworldly, lying here in this truck, in this alien landscape, with the full power of the gods above us. "My dad would have loved this."

I don't realize I've said anything until Nora shifts to cover my body with hers. Straddling my hips, she perches on my lower abdomen, and cups my chin between her palms. "He would be so proud of the man you are, Luke."

A complicated morass of emotions twists deep in my stomach. Would he? I'm a sex worker and a gambler. I haven't had a single long-term relationship since Mackenzie Lovette, and I live halfway around the world from my mom. I tell myself it's to make him proud, but how can that be?

"I don't think he would," I say, my voice so soft it's not even a whisper.

She pulls my face and locks her gaze with mine. "He would. Don't ignore how good you are. You're kind and strong and thoughtful. I can tell how much you love your mom, how much you still love him."

When I look into her eyes, all I see is truth and a future that's far brighter than any I should be entitled to. Is she right? How I wish she is.

I don't merely kiss her, I inhale her. In a single moment, we are locked together along every plane, and I am full of Nora. Nora. The hand at the base of her spine twists in her shirt, pulling her closer to me.

"Inside," she pants as I nibble down her throat and catch her nipple between my teeth. "I need you inside me. Please."

I need it, too. I pull a condom from the back pocket of my pants while she pulls down her leggings, exposing her naked self. Wicked, sexy woman, not wearing panties on our date.

"You're cold." With the setting sun, the temperature drops at least ten degrees, if not more.

"Warm me up, then." She spreads her legs, bold and open, her pussy glistening for me. I don't wait. I don't prep her the way I did before. She's wet enough. I give her what she wants.

She cries out as I ram into her, as she takes my full length, spasming around me. I almost come then, but I don't. My cheeks are wet, and I'm not sure why. Maybe it's this landscape. Maybe it's her.

"Luke." With her eyes open, she stares at the juncture where our bodies connect, watching as I pull out only to thrust back into her.

"Is this too much?"

"No." Her gaze meets mine, and it's full of heat and pleasure and steel determination. "More. Give me more."

I roll us over in the truck bed, our bodies still connected, but now she's on top of me, my cock spearing her the way I love. "Take whatever you need."

She props her hands against my chest and rocks her hips around my cock, swirling, exploring, finding the rhythm that works for her. When she finds it, she groans, squeezing me with the inner muscles of her pussy, milking me. "Yes. Fuck, yes."

"Sing for me, sunshine. Sing for me here, where it's just us and there's no one for miles to hear you scream my name."

I arch up into her, hitting her G spot, making her cry out my name. It echoes in the barren landscape, reverberating against the limestone formations.

Reaching between us, I use some of her juice to lubricate her clit and rub it in tight little circles. She breaks with a scream and an intense squeeze of her thighs around my hips, pinning me down as she seeks the last waves of her orgasm. As she finishes, her body becoming limp, I pump twice into her and release into the condom. My muscles are made of marshmallow and stardust.

"Perfect." I rub her back as she collapses onto my chest. "You're so perfect."

"It's you. It's all you, Luke. I've waited forever for you."

CHAPTER 24

THIS IS A DREAM. And a good one, not the nightmares I had for months after Pastor Curt tried to grope me.

This? This is bliss. Not just last night in the desert, staring out at the rocky pocked landscape with the Milky Way on full glorious display above us. This whole week, this whole trip is a too-good-to-be-true reverie. I'm simultaneously angry with myself for waiting so long and thrilled I waited for Luke.

I shouldn't get too attached. I know that. But the more I learn about him, the more I trust him with my body and my thoughts. The more I want him, all of him.

This is probably why I'm on my hands and knees right now as he rails me from behind. I thought I liked being on top, but from behind, with his hand twisting my hair? I could die happy from this alone.

He fucks me slow, over and over, bringing me to the edge

repeatedly, until every inch of me begs him. *"Make me come."* He hammers into me at an angle, each thrust hitting the bundle of nerves inside me. I'm close to shattering, but he doesn't do the one last thing that will make me climax.

"You like this, sunshine?" he asks. I can hear the smile behind his tone.

"More. Pull my hair. Tighter."

He does, and the strain is enough—no, too much, too good— and I climax, the pleasure spiraling up and out of control, leaving me limp, rocking me off my hands and landing face first on the mattress.

"May I finish?" His dick is still rock hard inside of me, and I squeeze him with my inner muscles. Thank you, Pilates. My entire body tingles.

"Definitely."

"Good." He rolls me onto my back then pulls my legs flush together. "Tell me if you don't like this." With my legs this close, he notches his sheathed cock between my thighs, the tip pointing toward my stomach. It's dirty and naughty and I fucking love it. I haven't seen him come yet since he's always been inside Latex, but I'm so curious. There's some feral part of me that wants to be covered with him.

"Take off the condom first."

He eyes me as if to gauge if I'm serious, but he knows by now that I am. Putting down my legs momentarily, he rolls the condom off his erection, then regains his position in front of me. I'm limp and fogged, but I lick my lips in antici-pation. Not that I have a lot of experience, but I'm a huge fan of Luke's cock. Seeing it between the muscles of my thighs as he works himself in, feeling his flesh against mine? If I could reach my clit right now, I'd probably orgasm again.

"This okay?" Luke holds my legs tightly, but I don't care. I like seeing him, his cock beaded with his liquid.

"Absolutely. I want to watch you come. I want you to

spray it all over me." Who am I and what have I done with Nora? Can't answer, I'm too busy having the time of my life.

"Anything for you, sunshine." He thrusts between my legs, skin against skin. He's hard and warm and I fucking love this. Before long, Luke's lower back tightens and arches, and a hot jet sprays across my belly.

Yes. This is what I want, to feel like he marked me. He already has. But as he releases onto me, all I feel is connected to him. I trust him. I want him.

I might—possibly, a little bit—love him.

THE DOORBELL RINGS as he cleans me with a warm washcloth. "Sorry about all of this." He won't look me in the eyes, so I run a finger down his cheek, drawing his attention. I will never tire of looking at him.

"Don't be sorry," I tell him. "I wanted it. I love it. It makes me feel close to you."

Smiling, he kisses my forehead and tosses the dirty washcloth in the laundry hamper. "I'll get the door. I'll only be a moment."

"Don't put pants on!" I call after him, but he doesn't listen. He pulls up his boxers as he crosses through the kitchen.

Boo. I should get up, too. At least to go to the bathroom.

I roll out of bed and then pause as I hear Luke's whispered "fuck."

Picking up his T-shirt from the floor, I pull it over my head and step into the kitchen. "Luke? Is everything okay?"

He's holding a printout in his hand and he stands so still it's like he is made of marble. I mean, he is, but this is different. He looks shattered.

Trepidation curls in my gut. "Luke?" Then I see the headline on the printout. It's an enormous headline, especially for an eight and a half by eleven sheet of paper. *Purity Princess Defrocked by Gigolo in International Scandal.*

All of the oxygen is sucked from the room. I can't breathe, can't stand.

"Nora?" Luke catches me a second before I collapse onto the floor, and the moment I'm in his arms, the tears come. "Are you okay?"

I can't talk for a long time as the sobs heave in my chest. Must be a combination of shock plus recent mind-blowing orgasm.

Luke hugs me to him, and I crash into his chest, into the warmth of him. "I'm so sorry," I finally say, rubbing my nose against the back of my wrist. "I made you all gross."

"I don't care." He rests his chin on the top of my head, but all this closeness only makes me more unsure.

I push him away and scramble to my feet. If only I'd put on underwear. It's difficult to take a stand with the wind against my vagina. "I do! I care. And now you know. Now you know who I am and what I am. Now you'll go off and tell the whole world how you fucked Honora Grand. It's a great story." It's been so many days since I thought of Honora, it feels strange coming out of my mouth. But we are two sides of one whole, after all. "I'm such a fool. I spent the last few days forgetting that you're my fake boyfriend. Pretending to be someone I'm not. And now you'll have to sign an NDA and—"

"I already knew you were Honora Grand." He stands in front of me, arms at his sides, the morning sunlight streaming across his chest in a way that was incredibly sexy not twenty minutes ago.

Now it only gives me a migraine. "You knew? What do you mean?"

His jaw clenches. "Giles told me."

"The pilot? Fuck, now I have to get him to sign an NDA—"

Luke grabs my hands, halting me mid-pace. "He's not going to say anything. I made him promise."

I pull my hands from his grasp and gesture wildly at the printout. Who even still uses the word gigolo? "Someone told! How do you know it wasn't him?"

"Because I trust him. And Asta sent this note." He holds up a Post-it note that says *Get your shit together ASAP. No one says Gigolo anymore.*

Despite my inner turmoil, I laugh. "She's direct, isn't she?"

"Yeah." He doesn't reach for me again, which I stupidly want. "Anyone could have seen us. The people at the bar? One of the delivery guys who saw you through the window? Look, I think I know who ratted us out." Sighing, he hesitates, then runs his hands through his hair, like he's ready to discuss something at last. "I'm going to tell you this, and you're going to think I'm an asshole. And I am. I know that. But I care about you, Nora. So I'm telling you this because I really value your trust."

Fuck, he's going to tell me that he's married or in a serial killer or something. How could I have been so stupid? He was probably just waiting to sell me out. It hurts my heart, but I cross my arms over my chest. I can rebuild my walls. "Okay."

His gaze meets mine, and his brown eyes plead with me to listen. "I'm a gambler. I owe a lot of money to some… unfortunate people, and I think they've been looking for me."

Oh.

 uke

I SHIFT from foot to foot, waiting for her reaction as she processes what I've said. Damn it, she looks way too good in my T-shirt. It's big on her, but the wide lower hem swishes around her legs, and all I want to do is push it up so I can kiss her pussy.

Not the time. Distracting myself from my problems with sex was how I got into this mess in the first place.

Nora clears her throat. "So, you gamble? Like a lot?"

"Not a lot. I wouldn't have started, but I needed money. My mom got sick. She needs this medicine, but it is obscenely expensive and the insurance...you know how it is. So I got into this poker game. I have the money." I drop my hands through my hair again. "I mean, I will have the money." Great going, remind her that she owes me money. What am I going to do, insist she leave it on the bedside table in C-notes?

She looks away, toward the Indian Ocean, visible through the living room window. She looks like she's thinking the same thing. "I—I can try to get you the rest of the money now. If you need. Then you won't have to—"

I know where she's going with this. "No, Nora, no. I don't want this week to be over. I don't need anything now, except to tell you what's going on. And to apologize. But please. Please don't think for a single second that I want any of this between us to be over." As I say it, it becomes even more true. Now that I've met her, I can't picture being away from her.

Tears dew at the corners of her eyes, glistening in the sunlight. "Am I in danger?"

"No." Tobias is an asshole, but he wouldn't hurt her. He knows the repercussions of messing around with someone so famous. If anything, he would try to blackmail her, which is still completely awful. I deflate. "I'm so sorry, Nora. I never should have put you in this position. I'll keep you safe. I promise. They won't find us."

She scrapes her toes against the light brown wooden floorboards, and the light scratching is the only sound in the room. What I wouldn't give for a grandfather clock of some sort. A ticking clock to toll my doom.

I'm getting too maudlin. I might be hypoglycemic.

"I trust you," Nora says softly, shaking me from my muse. "I do. And I don't want this week to be over, either."

Relief floods through me. "Okay. Great."

"I really like you, Luke." It's so quiet I'm not sure she even spoke, but it warms me up, just like the sunshine she is to me.

"I really like you, too, Nora." More than like, if I allow myself to be honest. But there's no place for that here.

I still don't move, but I watch as she flushes with pleasure, even her knees beneath the hem of my shirt.

"What do we about that?" She meets my gaze, and it's full of hope. I want that feeling, too. How do we only have two days? Not two weeks or two months or two lifetimes would be enough. A world without Nora seems sad indeed.

But I can't say any of this without sounding like a fracking asshole after I just told her how I need money.

So I go for something else. "First, I put on a shirt. Then we eat. Then, we go and have some fun."

While we can.

ora

I RUN my hand through my new asymmetric black bob. "I had no idea you were a hairstylist." The man thinks of every-thing. He ordered black hair dye and cut it for me in the bathroom sink before giving me the best massage I have ever had. Talk about a spa day.

"I am a man of many talents." He holds my hand and swings it between us as we walk toward the ferry terminal. "I thought it would be better incognito for you than to rely on the sunglasses and hoodie thing. You're not Clark Kent."

I grin, and while it has a lot to do with how much I like my new hairstyle—it makes me feel bold and powerful and edgy—it mostly has to do with Luke. I might be grinning like a sap and I could give a fuck.

This is fun.

Luke frowns at the ferry in front of us as we buy our

tickets and wait to board. "I don't know about boats. I'm not much of one for drowning at sea."

"Boats are awesome. Don't they have lakes in Wisconsin?"

"They do." He hands me a bottle of water. He's right, of course, about my disguise. Even though the ferry terminal isn't crowded, no one is paying any attention to us, except for this pair of young women who are eyeing Luke like he's a five course tasting menu at Noma. I shoot them dagger eyes.

"It's ironic that I'm a little scared of them," Luke says, ignoring the women and focusing the radiance of his attention on me. "Since my parents actually met on a cruise ship."

"Really?" My parents met at church, which is a well-publicized and very uninteresting fact.

"Yeah. My dad was an engineer, and my mom worked public relations. You know, people complaining about the internet access or wanting to change their rooms or whatnot."

"That's so cool. I've never been on a cruise. Yachts, yes." It's almost a relief that I know he knows about me. I don't have to hide anything, and it makes me like him even more. "Did they like it?"

"Oh yeah." He scuffs his toe against the floor of the ferry. "They worked together for years before my mom got pregnant with me, and even then, we traveled all the time when I was a kid. It's funny, thinking how they never would have met if they both hadn't had wandering feet."

"What do you mean?"

"My dad's from a coffee plantation in the Philippines, and my mom's from Menomonee Falls, but they traveled the world together. They didn't settle in Wisconsin until I was, like, five years old and my grandparents insisted I start school."

I link my arm with his and rest my head on his shoulder. "You learned from the school of life."

He laughs, a warm, soft sound that makes me tingle all over. "You could say that. What about you?"

Those girls across the way are now staring openly at Luke and giggling behind their raised hands. At least they're not taking photos. I've become a bit numb to it all over the years, but that unmistakable chirp of a camera snap haunts my dreams. After being outed, we can't be too cautious.

Still, they're more interested in Luke than me. He is here with me. For now he is mine.

"I was home schooled until middle school, when my parents wanted me to play a sport. But I'm awful at all organized sports. I kicked the ball into my own team's soccer net during my first gym class." My cheeks heat. "I've never told anyone that before."

"Why not?"

"My manager always wants me to present this invincible facade, like I magically sprung up a pop star before he 'discovered' me."

"I take it that's not how it happened."

"Hardly. How does anything happen? People don't really get plucked from obscurity. When my parents figured out I was terrible at sports, they shunted me into every single performing art they could find in our town. Ballet, jazz, tap, voice lessons, acting camp. Hell, I even took a stage fighting class one summer." I shake my head. "Fake swords are impossible."

"But you liked songwriting?"

My voice softens. "Yeah. More than I thought I would. My head goes quiet, and I forget all the things on my schedule when I'm writing. The only other time I feel like that is when I'm running, or, well—" I blush, holding back the statement of *when you're fucking me* but Luke grins like he knows exactly what I was about to say.

The ferry nears the coast of Rottnest Island, maneuvering

into position in the harbor. "I can't believe you really want to see them," I say.

He nudges me. "It's your own fault. If you hadn't shown me how cute quokkas are, I would have thought they were figments of imagination, like narwhals."

"Oh, Luke." I kiss his cheek, and the thrill of contact rushes through me. I really might love this man, even if he is totally wrong about narwhals. "Please tell me you're joking."

uke

THE LONGER WE go without someone talking to Nora, the more she seems to relax. Her disguise is working to make her more comfortable. Good. I like that she can be calm and free.

We get coffee from a restaurant near the quay and walk around downtown. "This island is beautiful," she says. "I see why people vacation here."

At that exact moment, a quokka of internet fame jumps onto a nearby picnic table and poses, its head tilted.

"That's wild." I laugh at the little creature as I snap a photo. It really is adorable, like a pudgy guinea pig had a decent shave.

Nora elbows me in the side. "I've heard they'll steal your coffee. Better watch it."

"Good point." It does seem to be eyeing my coffee cup with a not insignificant degree of interest. I scooch my very tasty beverage a few inches further away.

"Come on." I stand, extending a hand toward her. "Let's go explore the island."

WE RENT e-bikes from a nearby shop, since it's a twenty-three kilometer round trip. I might be in shape but I'm not a masochist.

Following the map from the bike shop, we pedal toward the nearby lighthouse, spotting quokka everywhere.

"Are we sure they don't have rabies?" Nora asks as we coast down the road, the wheels clacking as they spin.

"No animal that adorable can have rabies. They have to be sweet and lovable."

I can feel her eye roll, even though we are on totally separate bikes at least three feet from each other. "Have you never seen *Monty Python and the Holy Grail?*"

"I'm surprised you have."

"Why? Because I'm so chic and worldly?" She tosses her head.

"No, because it sounds like you spend your whole life working." I meant it as a joke, but from the chilly silence beside me, I said something unintentionally painful. "I'm sorry. I didn't mean it that way."

"It's okay. You're right." She rolls to a stop, straddling the bike with her toes on the ground. "I didn't realize until this trip how true that was. How they ran me minute by minute, until I was too exhausted, mentally and physically and emotionally, to question what was happening."

I don't say anything. I stop beside her like maybe my presence can comfort her. As an immense ego boost, it seems to work.

She scoffs and brushes a veil of tears from her eyes. "And I was supposed to be grateful. Grateful that I have at least three people counting my calories every single day. Grateful to be sewn into costumes night after night that smell like sweat and rotten foundation. Grateful to have a bodyguard because some producer once thought he'd check if that whole Purity Pledge thing was just an act."

Wait, what? My brain stalls, even as she keeps talking. I try to listen, but it's impossible through the haze of rage that just descended. I want to rip apart the world, find that asshole, and drive him into the ground with my fists. I'll bury him beside that fucker Pastor Curt.

Which, as someone who has never been in a fight before, is an odd sensation.

"I'm okay," she says quietly, reading something in my gaze I hadn't meant to say aloud. "All that stage fighting does translate. What I mean to say is, I'm supposed to be grateful for the fame and money and prestige. But at the end of the day, what I'm really grateful for is a charge in my laptop, butter on my toast, and this week with you. I choose this, Luke."

I close the distance between us and kiss her, holding the back of her head gently with one hand. She melts into my lips. Each brush of her against me sends spiraling warmth and pleasure through me. My mom would love this woman. I can picture her in my parents' backyard, me wearing a Kiss the Cook apron and manning the grill, while Nora and my mom laugh together over lemonade and making fun of me.

I want it. I want that vision to be real.

She breaks the kiss before I'm ready, instead wrapping her arms around my neck and pulling me into her embrace. "Oh, hey, look. Another quokka."

I am so fucked.

ora

WE ORDER PIZZA—VEGAN cheese for Luke— and curl up on the couch at the cottage together, looking through the photos on Luke's phone. I'm barefoot and lying mostly in his lap, but he doesn't seem to care. It's domestic and wonderful and I never want to leave this couch.

"I can't believe they don't fear humans," he says.

"That is very short sighted of them." I scratch the photo head of one of the quokkas that Luke somehow caught smiling. "It's the downside of no natural predators. They don't realize how quickly things can go from safe to bad."

"Social media will protect them. If anyone starts on an anti-quokka campaign, they'll immediately get cancelled."

"I don't think that's how cancellation works."

Luke picks up a piece of veggie pizza and plates it before handing it to me. "Do you ever worry you'll get cancelled?"

I pick at the cheese, which has cooled. "I'm not sure what

I would get cancelled for. I don't post strong political leanings, I back science, and I don't do drugs."

Luke's sigh feels like a waterfall against my back. "What about this?"

Oh. So it's this conversation. I shift off his lap, moving my plate to the table. If we're going to have this talk, I will do it face to face. "What about this?"

He glances away from me. He's sitting cross-legged on the couch, but he's tall enough that his feet hang over the edges of the cushion. "Me. People won't like that you had this week with me. And now the news is out, and someone called me a gigolo, which will definitely get back to my mom even though it's from a trash rag, and—"

"Is that all this is?" My breath feels like a lodestone inside my chest. "A week with you?"

He meets my gaze, and there's so much vulnerability in his unguarded expression that it feels like a gut punch. "That's what we agreed upon."

"But it's not what I want now." I'm not sure whether to touch him or stand up in a power pose, so I wrap my arms around my body, hugging myself. "I don't want this to be over. I'm not ready."

I'm not worried about being cancelled, or the anger my parents are undoubtedly feeling right now, not to mention Marvin, who I really think I'm going to fire when I get back to Sydney. "Before, I would wake up and feel like a commodity to be traded and paraded. With you, I feel like myself. I don't want to lose that. I don't want to lose you. I—I really care about you." Enormous understatement. He doesn't answer. He's still staring at the open pizza box, like that holds the secrets to life instead of heartburn. "Luke, I don't know what it would look like, me and you. I don't know where we would go or what we would do, but I do know that if I can be there with you, I'll be happy. I'll be at peace." I stare down at place where my arms crisscross my chest. I won't marry the baseball player, not for appearances or to keep the peace with my parents. I won't continue this ridiculous narrative about purity. I never believed it anyway. It was a way for my parents to control me, for Marvin to commodify me, and I'm done with it. I'll only be Honora Grand if I can be her on my own terms now.

That's pure. That's real.

A warm hand on my cheek calms my wandering thoughts. Luke leans his forehead against mine, and I match my inhalations and exhalations to his. "I want that, too. Nora. Very much. I'm not ready to let you go. I don't know how I'll ever let you go."

What follows feels like a dream. Our mouths meet, our tongues taste, hands are everywhere, hot and urgent. I'm on my back on the couch, my legs wrapped around Luke's head and neck as he devours me, making me cry out his name as I climax over and over. This. I want this, always.

We never say *mine*, but it's in our touch, our actions.

When Luke goes to get a condom, I stop him with a hand on his arm. "Please. This once. I want to feel you, all of you."

He pauses for a moment before sinking to his knees again before me and kissing me, the heat in his embrace enough to set me on fire. "Okay. For you. Only for you, Nora."

When he slides into my slick, hot, needy pussy, I can feel everything. Every ridge, the rubbery crown of him tapping deep inside me. "Yes." My eyes flutter closed, and I am a cloud of sensation. My body is ours by choice, joined together, rocking together. He shifts inside me to go deeper. A thousand sensations crowd my brain and it curls into want. *Yes. More.*

We speak but our words are a jumbled groan of want and need, pressure and demand, bites and nips and sucking.

When I climax, he is right there with me, releasing inside of me and it is the best I have ever felt.

We never say *love*. Not once, but it's there as we hold each other afterward, both of us trembling as the sex hormones work their way through us. *I am in love with Luke Bautista.*

"You want to sing, Nora?" Luke wraps his arms around me and pulls me against him, and I am whole. Complete. "You sing when my tongue is on your clit or I am so deep inside you, you wonder if I can split you open then weave you back together. You scream my name and you sing for me, sunshine. Always."

uke

MY PHONE BUZZES INCESSANTLY, demanding an answer even though there's nothing I would rather do than lie here beside Nora.

We progressed from the couch to the bed for rounds two and three. Now that I've gone raw with Nora, I might never go back as long as we are together. I hope that will be for a very long time.

My phone will not be stopped. It's practically whizzing itself off the bedside table. Moving as quietly as possible so as not to wake her, I pluck it from the table and head for the living room. I don't bother picking up my boxers from the floor. After last night, they seem superfluous.

With my mind wrapped up in Nora, I answer the phone without checking the caller ID.

"There you are, Bautista," Tobias growls into the phone.

Shit. That was a massive mistake. "Your money is on the

way, Tobias. I already sent you a down payment." It's a fraction of what I owe, but I should get credit for that.

"It isn't enough, is it? You said you'd make good. Interest is ticking up."

"Interest?" Okay, maybe I should have put on boxers for this conversation. I feel naked enough as it is. "It's a hundred grand, and I'm wiring the last of it to you tomorrow when I get it."

When he speaks, his voice is so slimy it makes me think of a lizard with a glandular problem. "That was before, Bautista."

"Before what?" But even as the words leave my mouth, I know. I know exactly what he's getting at, and it makes me want to rail and scream and break things.

"Before you hooked up with your little meal ticket."

Fuuuuck. My body simultaneously heats then ices over, my hand freezing into a fist at my side.

"Leave her out of this."

Tobias tsks at me like I'm a naughty boy in secondary school, the asshole. "Can't. You brought her into this. It's your fault. How would it look if I share what I know of you with the press?"

"I don't fucking care. Do whatever you want to me. Leave her alone." I grit my teeth and clench the edge of the kitchen island, so hard I wonder if I'll break the faux marble.

"I wonder how much she'd pay," Tobias says, musing. "To keep all this quiet. I mean, her fiancé can't be too happy about seeing that photo of you two together."

My brain skips like a needle jerking on a vinyl record. Fiancé? Photo of us together? *Fiancé?* I regret not investigating more about her on social media, but it seemed wrong, to get other people's views about her instead of her own. But fiancé?

Tobias laughs, a cruel, schoolyard bully kind of chuckle.

"Didn't you know about that? She's engaged, mate. To Bobby Nakamura. I'm sure you've heard of him. He plays for Milwaukee."

It's all I can do not to drop the phone. Why does this feel like Mackenzie Lovette all over again? Here I was, planning on how to introduce Nora to my mom and figuring out how to quit my job at Leather and Lace, and she's been engaged this whole time?

What was I? A practice round?

There's an explanation. I know there is. The woman I know wouldn't do this, not to me.

"Leave her alone," I tell Tobias. "I'll get the money to you today, within an hour, if you keep everything out of the news. And if I ever hear her name come out of your gruddy little mouth, I will cut out your tongue and feed it to the alligators in the Daintree River."

Tobias scoffs. "You're all bark and no bite, Bautista, but get me the money and I won't have to do anything rash. Also, fuck you, those are crocodiles in the Daintree, fuckwad." He hangs up, leaving me naked and alone in the kitchen with the onset of a killer migraine.

Where am I going to get eighty thousand dollars in the next hour? And why did Nora never tell me she is engaged?

CHAPTER 30

ora

How long have I slept? I don't particularly care. I stretch in bed, seeking out Luke's warm, steady body, but he isn't there.

Oh.

I wake up faster than I had intended, stroking the empty sheets where he had lain last night. It wasn't a dream, right? If I look in the shower, will I still see the imprint of my hands on the glass where I had to prop myself as he fucked me from behind? Then he soaped me up and cleaned me everywhere before bringing me back to bed. I love the way he takes care of me afterward, rubbing lotion into my sore spots, making sure I hydrate and eat.

Hmph. I had plans for today. I was going to wake up, nuzzle into him, and beg him to show me how he liked his cock sucked. I've never done that before, but after everything he's done for me, the least I can do is learn.

As I roll onto my side, I see a note from Luke on the

bedside table with my name on it. A little shot of pleasure runs through me at seeing his handwriting. He had to go out, but will be back shortly with coffee and breakfast.

Perfect man. Maybe I'll exercise. After all the sex, I could use a little yoga to limber me up. Then we can try out one of the positions I've only ever seen in Billie's *Kama Sutra*.

As I pull on my sports bra and leggings, I hear a knock on the front door, and every nerve in my body sparks to life. "Luke? Did you forget your keys?"

I probably shouldn't run to the door, but I'm too excited to wrap myself around him. This is what love is, apparently. Finding someone who makes me excited to face the day.

I pull open the door, and cold dread affixes me to the floor.

"Hello, Nora," my dad says.

MY MOTHER SITS on the couch, worrying her crucifix while my dad paces and rants. I guess Marvin couldn't be bothered to make the flight to Perth. "I can't believe you have been so irresponsible. Shacking up with this—this prostitute? Do you have any idea how worried sick Bobby Nakamura is? All these years, you've been so good. How could you blow it?"

My head throbs like there's an icepick behind my left eye. How dare they call Luke that? How dare they come here and demand anything of me? After all I have done for them, and what have they given me in return?

"Compliant, you mean," I say.

"I beg your pardon, young lady?" My dad's expression is a storm cloud before a category five hurricane.

"Compliant." I bite the word. "I've been compliant for years. I've gone along with all of your plans, all of your schedules, but I'm done. I'm not doing this anymore. And Bobby Nakamura can't be worried sick about me, because *we've never met.* He gives about as much shit about me as I do about him."

"Don't swear, Nora." My mother's voice is quiet, and when my dad glances her way, she immediately clams back up.

Enough of all of this. "Mom, I can swear if I want to. How did you two even find me? I turned off my phone and all the geo-location services."

My dad preens like he's the winning lawyer about to get a snake oil salesman off. "It was easy enough after that article came out. You can't even imagine the damage control Marvin and his PR department had to do to keep that under wraps." Yes, I can, and cannot muster even one single care. "Once the private investigator talked to Billie, we put several clues together, and here we are. Those social media candids weren't even necessary."

"What?" In all honesty, I had been tuning out of his la-la-la-I'm-so-great spiel, but this draws my attention. "What social media candids?" Something else he mentioned has also now sparked a deep sense of unease. "And what about Billie? She's okay, isn't she?" I suppose now that they've found me, I can turn my phone back on. I've been a total shit friend for not checking in with her, and I hope she'll understand. She won't if my asshole parents fired her.

My dad's phone rings, and he answers it, turning toward the window. Completely ignoring my question, by the way. Thanks, Dad.

"Mom?"

At my query, my mom looks up from the hole she's staring into the floorboards, but she doesn't stop rubbing the crucifix between her fingertips. "Yes?"

"Is Billie okay?"

"Oh." My mom doesn't meet my gaze. "You understand, of

course you do. We had to fire her. She knows the deal, after all, and this is her fault."

"No, it's not."

My dad ends his call. "Don't raise your tone with your mother, young lady."

"Are you fucking serious?" I can't sit still for this, so I stand and pace in front of the kitchen island. "I'm not fifteen any more. I'm not a child you can control. This is my body and my life and I am not going to listen to any of this shit anymore!"

Both my parents' jaws hang open, and my dad's expression is so toxic it should come with a hazard symbol. But this feels right.

"I've wasted too long trying to live up to your impossible standards, and at the end of the day the only one who has to live in this body is me. So from this point on, the only one who has a say in how I live is going to be me. I'm writing the songs I want to sing. I'm surrounding myself with people who lift me up. I'm not going to be a poster child for something I don't believe in. No more."

"What about money?" My dad sneers a little on the last word. "You'll need it soon enough. We control your finances."

"Not all of it."

His eyes narrow and his jaw sets into a harsh line. Maybe I shouldn't have told him, but I'm past caring. "After what you spent on this ridiculous week? God sees what you did, and He will punish you."

"I think God wants me to live the best life possible, full of love and compassion and caring for other human beings. That's what I'm doing. I'm not hurting anyone by having sex with Luke." I get dangerously close to saying I love Luke, but I catch myself. Saying it aloud isn't a weapon. It's a gift, and it doesn't belong to these people. There's only one person who deserves to hear it from me.

"Except for us," my dad replies, turning toward my mother and taking her limp hand. "You don't care at all what you're doing to us, you ungrateful child."

This is tedious. I won't convince them. Not now, maybe not ever. "I'm done with this conversation. You've held me in a weird thrall for years, and it ends today. I have to go find Luke."

Without looking at either of my parents, I grab my phone and a set of house keys, and I make good and damn sure to slam the door behind me.

uke

"I was wondering when I'd hear from you," Asta says over the phone. Thank fuck she doesn't insist on video chatting. I'm in no condition, but after the hour I've had, she's my last chance.

"Sorry I didn't check in earlier." I run my hands through my hair as I walk down the beach. The Indian Ocean is calm today, the waters so clear I wouldn't even need a snorkel, but it's not helping my mood. I want to get back to Nora, but only once I figure out how to get Tobias off her back.

"Is everything going well?" It's almost like I can hear her checking tick boxes on her ever-present tablet. If I were more like Asta, I wouldn't have gotten into this mess. Or maybe I would have anyway. Being more organized wouldn't have prevented my mom's medical bills piling up or my dad's unexpected death.

"Yeah. It's—it's going really great." I flash back to a picture of Nora beneath me as I tuck a curl of hair behind her ear. The way she threw her head back when we were coasting on Rottnest Island, like she's drawn to the sun like a flower.

"Hmm." There's a clicking sound, like she's tapping the end of a ballpoint pen. "What's wrong?"

It's best to be direct with Asta. "I need the money early. An advance. You can take some of it as collateral or interest or whatever."

Asta sighs. "What the fuck did you do?"

"Nothing. Nothing, I swear."

"Is that why you're trying to get paid early? Because you did nothing? Is the client disappointed?" There's that dominatrix streak to her tone that, I have to admit, thrills me a little.

"I mean, I did the job." And maybe fell in love, a little bit, but Asta doesn't need to know that. "She's satisfied. I'm sure of it."

"If I call her directly, is that what she'll say?"

"Of course." I hope. I'm eighty-eight percent sure, but if Nora finds out Tobias might blackmail her, that's probably it for the two of us. Which hurts far more deeply than I had anticipated, though not as much as hearing about her fiancé. I thought I had learned that falling in love only leads to heartbreak, but apparently I am as naïve as a quokka.

"Hmm," Asta says again. There's a long pause. "How much trouble are you in?"

I sit down on the beach and dig my toes into the sand, letting it cover my sandals. Asta does not condone gambling, and while it's not like I was doing it while on the job, she won't be thrilled. "A hundred grand."

"You're a fucking idiot." Her exhale is so loud I feel its reproach throughout my entire body. Even staring out at the ocean can't cleanse me. "Do you promise you didn't do anything foolish? I'm not going to hear you've fallen in love or some shit like that, am I? I've seen the photos."

My stomach curls on itself. Maybe I should have eaten first. "What photos?"

"I'll send them to you. They're all over social media. You and Honora Grand on a ferry outside Perth. Riding bikes by a lighthouse. It's cute, like some romcom montage."

Shit. It's out. I hope Nora's okay. The minute Asta agrees to help me out, I can do damage control for Nora. "Then you know I'm doing my job."

"Just don't quit on me. Please? You're the best romance expert I've got at the moment."

Yet that's exactly what I was pondering, how to quit, what I will do with my life once I get out of the biz. I'm pretty sure a commercial airline will accept my resume, but maybe that's not something I would want, to be away from Nora like that. Does she even want me if she paid me five hundred grand? Maybe I should offer to give the rest of the money back. All this is moot unless she isn't actually marrying Bobby Naka-mura, who, yes, I do know, and he's fucking gorgeous and talented and rich. The bastard.

Still, this is all a self-indulgent fantasy if I don't get the money to Tobias by the end of the hour. "I'm not going to quit, Asta. I love my job. Nora is a client, that's all. Once our week is up, it's up. We'll part happy and she can go back to her real life." Ugh, why does that feel so callous? Besides, she's the one who is apparently engaged and didn't see fit to tell me. All of that tenderness, all of her understanding and telling me how proud my dad would be, she didn't mean it. She couldn't have.

At the end of the day, we are not simply Luke and Nora. We are a sex worker and the Silver and Gold Goddess. Trust me, I know how that story ends.

"All right. I'll wire the money wherever you want. No fee

since this is the first time you've ever asked me for a favor, but don't let it become a habit. It's so tedious."

I'm so relieved I collapse into the sand, knowing it's going to be hell to get out of my hair later. "Thanks, Asta. I'll text you the wire info."

She hangs up without saying goodbye, but that's not a problem. Thank fuck. She barely chastised me, I don't need to tell Nora about Tobias's latest threat, and as soon as that wire transfer goes through, I'm free.

I don't hear the footsteps through the sand until small, bare feet stand beside my head. "Nora?" I sit up so quickly, a dizzy spell rolls through me. "Are you okay?"

"What was that about?" Her voice is soft, like she's either pissed or sad, and both make me feel like an asshole.

Honesty is probably for the best. "Asta. I called and asked her for an advance."

"Why?" She's standing just a little too far away from me.

"Tobias, the guy I owe money to, he said he would blackmail you if I didn't pay him immediately and in full."

"Why didn't you just ask me?"

This is not a conversation I wish to be having while lying in a pile of sand and seabird poo. "I don't know. I didn't want you to think poorly of me." I didn't want to remind her of the money she paid for this week. I wanted to pretend this was real. It never could have been, not if she's engaged.

She falls to her knees in the sand beside me. "I couldn't think poorly of you. Not for a moment."

"Nora—" Behind her, a crowd gathers, their phones out and at the ready, and everything in my body twists into tight little pretzel-shaped knots. What am I doing? I'm not doing what I should, and that's my job. It will be the last way to protect her. It will be easier for her if she doesn't know how much I love her. Damn it. I know better than to fall in love with a client. "Nora, I don't think we should do this."

"Why not?" The surprise on her face hurts so much, but it's about to get worse. I want to take her hands, but if I do, I might not say what I have to say.

"Because you're engaged."

Her brow furrows, like she has completely forgotten this fact, but to me, it's Mackenzie Lovette all over again. Poor Luke, falling head over heels only to come in second. I'm not the long term guy. I'm the placeholder, the fuckboi.

"No, Luke, you don't—"

"I do understand. I know who I am. I know what I do for a living. Your fans?" I gesture toward the crowd around us, keeping my voice low. Even now, I have to protect her. "They don't want to see you with me. They want you with someone famous, someone at your level. This could ruin you."

Tears well up in her eyes, and I move closer to shield her from the cameras. "I don't care," she says softly.

"I do." And I mean it, on so many levels. I care about her, and what happens to her, and how much I am about to hurt her. But it's for the best. What kind of future can a sex worker and a pop star have together?

None, especially when I see her dad storming down the beach toward us, cutting through the crowd like a scythe.

"I care about you, Nora." So much. *Care* is an inadequate word for what I feel. I take her hand in mine and squeeze it, burning the memory of her into my skin. "And that's why I need to leave."

CHAPTER 32

N̄ora—a few days later

I STEP off the plane from Australia, a parental harangue-induced migraine throbbing behind my eyes. Who knew there were so many different ways for them to call me a slut? I didn't even have Dawson as a buffer, since the coward needed to stay behind in Sydney for some business meeting I suspect he invented.

My mother slides her arm through mine, but it's less a gesture of camaraderie and more a vise to make sure I don't run away. "The car is waiting, dear. This way."

The sunlight in Los Angeles hurts my eyes, even with my overlarge designer sunglasses to hide the dark circles. It feels like last week with Luke was a dream. Did I even lose my virginity? After the nonstop lectures I endured from my parents, it suddenly seems entirely possible that none of it happened.

My mother even brought that up. That if I abstain long

enough, I'll be a virgin again. Which is not how physiology works.

Even if they want to erase the memory of him, I can't. I miss him in a very deep part of my being, one that keeps churning like I'm about to be ill.

I can't get in this car. I can't repeat this pattern. If I follow my parents, I will commit myself to a life of toxic shame. It will be like erasing Luke.

My mom pulls on my arm to get me into the waiting SUV, but I pull my arm from hers. "No. I'm not going with you."

My father sighs so loudly it's almost like he's exhaled a cumulonimbus cloud into the clear blue sky. "Nora, we have discussed this."

"Yes. On and on and on and I need a break. I will see you later. Maybe."

I turn on one heel and head straight for the taxi line. Whether people recognize me or don't want to get in the way of my Godzilla-esque rampage, the crowd parts and I slip directly into the next available cab.

WHEN THE DOOR to her condo opens at my third knock, I burst into tears. I can't help it. Too many emotions combined with jet lag and grief overwhelm me.

Billie wraps me in her arms and holds me tightly. "Oh, Nora."

"I am so sorry. I'm such an asshole. I am an awful friend. I got you fired." The words come out in hitching sobs.

"You're only an asshole if you don't tell me how it was with Hot Guy." She doesn't let me go. "And you didn't get me fired. Marvin Strong's undisguised misogyny fired me. I'm okay."

I hold her more tightly, feeling more grounded than when the plane landed forty-five minutes earlier.

"Come inside," she says softly. "Let's talk. Oh, honey, I love your hair."

SHE WRAPS me in a bright teal cashmere throw and makes me a cup of peppermint tea.

"I really am sorry." I sniffle into a massive ball of facial tissues. "I shouldn't have shown up here."

"Yes, you should have." Billie sits beside me and tucks her bare feet under the hem of the throw. "I have been dying to know what's been going on with you."

"I should have called." I can't shake this feeling of being a jerk, a terrible friend. "I'm sorry, I had my phone off so I couldn't be tracked, and they found me anyway."

"I get it." She shrugs. "Seriously, how was it?"

I sigh into a facial of peppermint tea steam. "Amazing. No, amazing doesn't quite cover it."

Billie whistles, a playful gleam in her eyes. "Ooh, girl got dickmatized."

"I did not get dickmatized. Wait, what does that mean?"

"It's when the sex is so good, you can't think of anything else." She nudges my hip with her toes. "Mesmerized by the big D."

"I mean, the—the sex was excellent." It feels weird but also wonderful to talk about it at last, like it really happened. After the last thirty hours of my parents slut shaming me, I need this. "It made me realize what I've been missing."

"No, Nora. You haven't been missing sex like that." Billie sips her own mug of tea. "You missed all the mediocre stuff. All the teenaged premature ejaculators or college boys who can't find your clit even with very detailed GPS navigation.

You went from zero to three sixty, to play in the big leagues. You're lucky, girlfriend."

I ponder this for a long moment. She's right, of course she is.

"The question, though, is was it just sex?" Billie's question cuts through my rapidly encroaching fatigue. "It's totally normal to confuse sex with feelings, especially when you don't have a lot of experience. I fell *hard* for the first guy who really got my body, but when I woke up from the orgasm hormones, I realized he was a total asshole."

"Luke isn't an asshole. Definitely not." Yes, the sex was incredible, and it was a totally different experience, finally living my own life. But I don't think I've confused sex for feelings. Even now, when my eyes seem to be shutting from their own volition, I wish he were here beside me, making me laugh or talking about his family. Is that the same thing? "I don't know what to do, Billie."

"Okay." She takes the mug from me and places it on the coffee table. "First, you need a nap. We can work out the rest of your life later."

Later. All I can think of as I drift off to sleep is that I hope Luke can be included in later.

CHAPTER 33

*L*uke—*One Month Later*

"Honey." My mom stands at the foot of the couch. She's thinner than she ever has been before, but since she started the treatments two weeks ago, she also has a bit of color in her cheeks. "It's not that I don't love having you here. And you've been a huge help." Ha. I went to the grocery store once and that was primarily because we ran out of beer and I was craving Spotted Cow. "But what exactly are you doing?"

"I'm helping." I arc the remote control around her slender frame to pause the Scandinavian crime show I've been binging.

"Right." She stares dubiously at the evidence of my depression, which is currently littering the floor. "Could you maybe help by getting a job? Or at least picking up some of this trash from the floor?"

I grumble and sit upright, disturbing the bag of neon orange-colored chips I'd perched on my chest. Say what you will about the Midwest, but we have the world's best snack foods, particularly if one has been called a prostitute, a home wrecker, and the Architect of Purity's Destruction. Just to name a few.

After the first few days, I stopped reading the headlines and removed social media from my phone. Asta told me to take a break and pull my shit together, and so I have ended up here, the place I've been trying unsuccessfully to escape since my dad died.

This house is so full of memories, every time I turn a corner, it feels like they punch me in the chest. There's the vase my mom always used when my dad used to bring her home the day lilies she loves. That's the pan that's a bit wonky on one side from the time when my dad experimented with making homemade candy canes. That table that's chipped on one side? He was showing me how to ride a bike, but there was a snowstorm outside, so he pushed me in our living room and right into the edge of said chipped table. I still have the little divot scar on my left shin.

On the other hand, being here and surrounded by him has been more cathartic than I expected. I can remember all the good things about my dad, not just the grief after his death. It's brought me and my mom closer, too. Simply eating dinner together at the same table night after night has made me feel more grounded. I've taken her to her doctor's appointments, and gotten a much clearer picture of her illness and trajectory than I could from continents away. It's different, having a routine.

Still, boredom and grief don't quite cover how I've been feeling. I can't even get my dick interested in a little tug session after my mom's gone to bed.

Besides my dad, all I think about is Nora.

It was the right decision, pushing her away. I'm mostly certain of that. I just wish it didn't hurt so much. I'd gotten closer to her than anyone else in ages and none of it makes me feel better right now.

So I've chosen the couch and chips and very good local beer. Like a man.

"I'll clean up." I kiss my mom's cheek and head down the hall to the kitchen to get a trash bag.

"I'm changing the channel," my mom calls. "I don't know how you can watch this maudlin stuff. It's so dark. Literally."

"It suits my mood," I grumble to myself, pulling a trash bag from the discount store-sized roll in the closet. What could Nora be doing now?

Not me, that's for sure.

In my defense, I could call, but what can a person say over the phone? Especially if she's under the control of her very intense family?

Oops, sorry I didn't tell you I'm madly in love with you. Like that will go over well.

When I return to the living room, my mom has turned on one of those late afternoon talk shows, where the host is a charming actress who was popular in the early 2000s with a too-wide smile, and the music is loud enough to cut through the three pm doldrums.

My mom points to the TV. "I love Cordy Chandler. She was so good in that show when you were a kid."

Far be it from me to begrudge my mom her guilty pleasures. I toss trash into the bag, not really listening to the woman's voice or the intro music.

That is until the woman announces, "Welcome to the set, Honora Grand!"

What. The. Fuck? Like I'm spinning in quicksand. I turn toward the TV and indeed, there she is. My Nora. Her hair black and short, like the cut I gave her before we took the ferry to Rottnest Island, but a little fuller and more stylish. She wears four-inch stilettos, a blousy hunter green peasant top, and black jeans that cup all the curves I've tried so hard to forget.

"Turn it off," I tell my mom. Nora laughs at something the host says, tossing her head back, her hair grazing her shoulders. I don't want to watch this with my mom. It's a two in the morning, one-six-pack-deep kind of thing. One where I can let my cock out to play while I remember how good I had it for a few days.

My mother crosses her arms over her chest, holding the remote hostage. "Absolutely not. You need to see her. I love you, Luke, but you can't hide out here forever. She's famous. Grammys and supermarket tabloids famous. You cannot avoid her forever, and this is a baby step."

I sink onto the couch, the trash bag falling open between my knees. I probably should not have gotten drunk a month ago and told my mom everything. Moms never forget.

"So, Honora, you've been in the news a lot lately." The host tosses back her head of artfully dyed auburn curls. "What do you want to say?"

Onscreen, Nora stares into the camera, and it's like she's staring directly at me. "It's no one's business what I do with my body and my life. I spent far too long under the illusion that I owed someone for my life, but it isn't true. I worked hard to get where I am. And I owe that realization to one very special man."

The camera cuts away from her and it takes every ounce of strength inside me not to wrestle the TV into submission.

The host arches one perfectly sculpted eyebrow. "A very special man? I've heard tales from Marvin Strong about Bobby Nakamura." The audience whoops like eight year olds on a playground. My stomach tightens and curls.

"Actually, Cordy, in all honesty, I've never met Bobby Nakamura. I'm sure he is a lovely person, but he's not for me. Marvin Strong and I have also parted ways." Nora gestures off stage, where I presume someone is waiting. "I have a new manager now, Louise Fields. I'm making a lot of changes in my life."

Cordy's dark brown eyes widen. "Hopefully not giving up music? Your songs speak to so many people. They've definitely gotten me through some rough times." The audience oohs in apparent commiseration.

"No, I'll never give up music." Nora's smile is soft. "But I need to fight for what I want."

"I like her." Somehow my mom has ended up on the couch beside me, and she punches my shoulder gently with her fist. "She's got moxie."

I'm having difficulty processing any of this. Nora on screen, my mom beside me. What does all this mean and why oh why did I eat so many deep fried cheese curds? Damn self-flagellating lactose intolerance.

'This song is for him," Nora says, standing from her chair. A production assistant brings out a guitar and hands it to her.

"I've heard it's pretty racy." Cordy's eyes twinkle as my insides tie themselves into very complicated Gordian knots.

"It's about purity, and the best man I've ever met." Nora's voice cuts through the TV waves and hits me straight in the heart. "He knows who he is. I want him to know how much I love him."

CHAPTER 34

mpure

THERE'S a kaleidoscope of sunsets overhead
  Painting our skin in this pickup bed
  With you

YOU TASTE OF ARABICA, smell like the sea
  As far as I go, nowhere I'd rather be
  Than with you
  With you.

IN THIS MOMENT
  I'm a diamond, flawless
  We aren't lawless

. . .

Tangled
    In a moonlit desert
    On the far side of the world

THEY'VE BEEN TELLING me and telling me what to feel
    But the only time I've really felt real
    Is with you.

THERE'S a love that takes and a love that gives
    But here in the night I see choices aren't sieves
    With you
    With you

I NEVER WANTED to be perfect
    Bleached and dried and posed
    With your quokka's smile
    You opened doors I thought were closed
    So tarnish me
    Tarnish me
    Tarnish me, burnish me, polish me
    Again and again and again and again and again

'CAUSE in this moment
    You're the key to my soul
    Touch me I'm whole

I'D GIVE it all for you
    Unlock the chain around my...
    Heart

. . .

I KNOW this is only one brilliant moment
    In the thousands we both endure
    Of all the things I've seen in this world
    I know one thing for sure.
    How can true love ever be impure?

CHAPTER 35

ora

"Premiering first on Cordy Chandler's *Early Evening Show,*
'Impure' soars to the top of the charts." Louise finishes
reading the headline from her phone with a magnificent
flourish. "Perfect. Just perfect."

Beside me in the car, Billie squeezes my hand. "Are you
ready for this?"

I stare out the window of the SUV at the unassuming
white and red ranch-style home, with a large oak tree in the
front yard. It's a nice house, the kind of house my family
owned before my first song, "Schoolgirl Crush," went viral.
No, this is nothing like the sterile two-story clapboard house
where I grew up. This looks like a well-loved kind of home,
and it makes it easier for me to open the door, letting in the
crisp Wisconsin fall air. There's an old tire swing in the front
yard and hydrangeas line the wall. "Yeah. I'm ready. Wait
here."

I cross the yard with the dried husks of leaves crunching beneath my feet. Maybe this isn't a good idea. There's a very real, very distinct possibility Luke didn't hear the song or watch the show, but his mom had said—

There is no place right now for indecision. I miss him. So much that my whole body tingles without him, and the closer I get to this door, with its friendly twig wreath adorned with bright orange pumpkins glued on top, the more I feel drawn to him.

I knock on the door, the hard wood unyielding under my knuckles. It's only been a few weeks, but so much in my life has changed, and I'm ready for more.

I only hope that Luke is, too.

A small woman with graying brown hair and pale skin, wearing a long maroon-colored cardigan, answers the door and breaks into a smile. "I knew it would be you. Hi, honey."

There's something about this woman that makes me want to get to know her, but also I feel like I already do. "Hi, Mrs. Bautista. I'm Nora Grandin."

She laughs, a crisp clear sound that rings in the autumn air. "Like I don't know? He's missed you. Come on in."

The house smells like a combination of empanadas and freshly baked cinnamon apples, but not in that chemical way of air fresheners. Stepping into Luke's childhood home feels like arriving somewhere I know I will be safe and happy and cared for. It's similar to wrapping myself in blankets on the couch with a hot cup of cocoa and marshmallows beside me. Of course he would have grown up here.

"Luke!" His mom calls. She has the same shape of her eyes that Luke has, but from the photos of his dad on the mantle, I can see who had the most influential genes. His dad was handsome and had an innate liveliness that leaps out of his photograph. Just like Luke. "Get your ass down here."

"Coming, Mom!"

His voice scratches every nerve ending under my skin, my whole body attuned to it. I'm caught between wanting to run as far and fast as I can, and waiting until I can launch myself into his arms. Hopefully that's how this turns out. Hopefully he doesn't turn away or say no.

As if sensing my indecision, his mom rests a warm hand on my back. "Don't worry. We heard your song. I never could have dreamed someone would make my boy get all teary eyed, but you did. Well done. There's been way too much Bill Withers in this house. Luke needs to be a little shaken up from time to time."

Then he's here, in a flurry of activity, like he was mid-Parkour when his mom called him. There's a thousand pound weight in my chest, but at the same time, my heart feels light and soaring. He's as handsome as I remember, even if he is wearing old high school sweatpants and a black T-shirt one size too small.

He skids into the living room on bare feet, his jaw slack and eyes wide. "Nora."

"Hi, Luke." I wave like a fool, because shyness has engulfed me and I have a sudden need to run away.

"For heaven's sake, you couldn't have worn a shirt that fits?" His mom goes to him, taps his cheek fondly, then turns to me. "I'll make some tea for all of us. You two talk."

When she leaves the room, everything I had planned to say follows her on her heels.

Luke straightens, stuffing his hands in the pockets of his sweatpants, which really only serves to accentuate the muscular lines of his chest. Desire and memory swirl around my lower spine. "What are you doing here?" he asks.

His question is entirely pertinent. What am I doing here? It all made sense when I worked it out with Louise and Billie earlier this week.

He nods toward the TV. "I saw you yesterday on Cordy Chandler."

I can't think of anything to say to this. "Yeah."

Ugh, why is this so awkward? When I thought about this moment, there was more hugging and kissing and catching up. It wasn't me, standing in his very comfortable living room with the scent of cinnamon apple tea wafting from the kitchen.

He runs a hand through his hair for one heart-stopping motion, then sticks his hands back in his pockets. "You wrote a song about me."

"Yes." My pulse throbs in my neck, sending a flush throughout my body.

"About me deflowering you."

He says it in his normal octave, which I assume means he's come out to his mom. A thrill of pleasure runs through me. He's told his mom about me. "Yes."

"You sang it on Cordy Chandler. And apparently now it's one of the most popular songs in the US."

"Yes."

He tilts his head to one side. "Don't you regret it? You've just told the entire world that you are no longer a virgin. And I'm the one who did the deed." He sighs. "What are people going to think?"

"I don't care. I don't regret a single second. I wrote that song because I want you to know how much I care about you. I wrote it so the world would know that you are valued for exactly who you are. I wanted you to be seen. The whole thing about a purity pledge... To my parents, it's about following some arbitrary rule and outdated, barely covert misogyny. But that's a myth. It's right and clean and honest to embrace who you are and what you want with a whole heart, and to treat others with respect. So this song is my new purity pledge. To live my life on my own terms."

Luke is quiet for a long time. "That's a good resolution."

I close my eyes and take a deep breath. Time to let it all out. "I miss you. So much. I hate the way we left things."

When I open my eyes, Luke stands before me, close enough to touch but not yet touching.

"Me too," he says.

At my side, my hands clench into fists and then I relax them, stretching my fingers wide.

"I can't believe you wrote a song about me." His smile is uncertain, but pleased.

"That's probably weird."

"No. It was nice." His words sound hollow here in the living room, beside photos of his parents in their cruise line uniforms. They look so happy. "How are you here? I assumed you were in New York."

"Not anymore." I desperately need this conversation to be less awkward. He's still so close but not against me. Not where I need him to be. "Luke, I love you. So much. I've been making a lot of changes in my life. I want you to be a part of them, in whatever capacity you're comfortable with. I know it's a lot, and I'm a lot, and my schedule is crazy and—"

"Yes." I'm not sure if he actually says it or it's just that his gaze catches mine and holds it, hunger and hope burning like embers deep in his dark brown eyes. "I love you, too. This last month has been fucking torture. Yes."

"Yes?" I close the distance another centimeter and his mouth is a breath from mine.

He doesn't answer with words, but with his lips, crashing into me with all the pent up want I've felt for the last few weeks. I wrap my arms around his neck, joyful, light, and he swings me around the living room, not releasing me from his embrace. I'm full and free.

He breaks the kiss and cups my jaw in between his hands,

strands of my hair bristling under his touch. "Come and meet my mom."

Smiling like a complete and utter happy fool, I slip my hands into his and squeeze. "Gladly."

uke

I CAN'T BELIEVE we are sitting here at my family's worn kitchen table, the one we bought for ten dollars at a garage sale in Door County when I was eight. Yet we are on our third cup of cinnamon apple tea, and I haven't seen my mom this animated in years. Part of it is the new meds, but most of it is Nora.

"So then Chris Mulroney picks up Cree Wallander in a fireman lift and twirls him around on the dance floor," Nora says through bouts of giggles. "It was so funny."

My mom slaps the table. She's laughing so hard, her cheeks are bright red and her eyes sparkle. "Nora doll, you have the best stories. I don't think I'll ever get tired of hearing them."

Nora picks up another one of my mom's famous brownie cookies. "I don't think I'll ever get tired of these cookies, Mrs. Bautista."

My mom scoffs loudly. "Please. Call me Tara. And I will make you these any time you like." She stands from the table, picking up her tea cup and bumping me with her hip. "If you two young people will excuse me, I need a brief nap, and then I will pretend to have a dinner date with a friend so you two can have some time to work things out."

I watch as my mom maneuvers around the kitchen and down the hall toward her bedroom.

"Your mom's amazing." Nora turns to me and pops the last bite of her cookie into her perfect mouth.

"She likes you." That admission warms me from the inside out. She never liked Mackenzie, but Nora? She's welcomed her with open arms. "Me, too."

Nora's smile blossoms across her face. "Has it been good to be home?"

I pick up one of the cookies and tear it in half, handing a portion to her. "Definitely. We've talked a lot. I finally told her about my job, so she knows everything."

"What did she say?"

"She told me she was really proud of me, and that my dad would be really proud of me. Then she said he'd kick my ass for gambling and lying about it." I laugh. It's felt so good to let go of all the worry. "She told me she was glad I was seeing the world and making people happy, but that I needed to be happy myself. I guess she saw those pictures of us together. She kept dropping hints about you, sending me commercials with your songs as the soundtrack, or the videos and memes of you from your Super Bowl halftime show. Killer costume, by the way." She had been dressed in a miniskirt with so much silver and gold spangle she had barely needed a spotlight.

Nora rolls her eyes. "Do you have any idea how long it took me to get into that? I picked glitter out of my butt for the next month and a half."

I arch an eyebrow, picturing her naked body shimmering with glitter. It's a very pleasant image, but doesn't quite fit with this pockmarked table in my family's cozy kitchen. Or maybe it does. "Come on. It was worth it."

She looks as though she is about the shake her head, but then grins. "It was. I mean, it was the Super Bowl. Talk about living the dream."

"I thought you liked tiny open mic nights in places with sticky floors."

She considers, tilting her head to one side. "I like that, too. But the Super Bowl was fun. My parents don't normally drink, but that night they got completely obliterated, so my friend Billie and I snuck out and went to one of the after parties. It was pretty epic, even if I did head back to the hotel by eleven. I was way too tired to stay up later." She hesitates for a second then reaches across the table and takes my hand. "Maybe next year we can go together? Or to the Kentucky Derby? I've never been. My mom is scared of horses."

"I'll bet you look amazing in a fascinator." I squeeze her hand, then lean over to kiss her cheek. "Anywhere. I'll go anywhere with you."

"Good." She flushes. "Maybe your mom can come, too."

"I'd prefer the Derby!" My mom calls down the hallway. "A few more months and I'll out-mint julep anyone!"

Nora catches my gaze and we both dissolve into laughter. It feels good, right, to be here with her.

She glances over my shoulder. "You look a lot like your dad."

"Thanks." He would have loved Nora. I follow the direction of her gaze to see the picture of my mom and dad on their wedding day. They're standing in the chapel of the cruise ship where they met, the captain between them. "You know he asked her to marry him after only three dates? He said he knew right away."

Like me. I think I knew immediately that Nora is the one. The only.

I glance down at our hands, our fingers entwined together right above the spot where I carved my initials into the worn wood of the kitchen table. "Nora, one thing I still don't understand. That night, at the auction? You could have chosen any one of those men. Why did you pick me?"

She leans her head toward me, resting her forehead on mine. I have never felt so relaxed and happy in my entire life. To breathe the air she does, it's more than I ever could have hoped for. "I chose you, Luke Bautista," she says, her voice soft so my mom doesn't hear us. "Because I knew even then that you were the only man worth getting to know. And I was right. I want to spend a lifetime learning every little thing about you."

"Same." I capture her lips with mine and sink into the luxury of her kiss. Who says a gambler can't get lucky?

EPILOGUE

*N*ora—*One Year Later*

My KNEE JIGGLES repeatedly up and down as the plane circles over the turquoise waters off the coast of Queensland. We need to land, like, yesterday. I still have a thirty minute drive from Proserpine to Airlie Beach, but if our luck holds, Luke will be there to meet me. And it's been far too long since I've seen him.

"Wheels down in ten," the pilot says through my headset. It was either charter this private plane to the Whitsundays or fly in the private jet of a friend, who is notorious for never being on time. Pass. I'd rather chance it on a puddle jumper than miss another hour of seeing Luke.

After an uneventful landing, I deplane so quickly I barely have time to thank the pilot, but it doesn't matter. None of it does.

Because there's Luke, holding an enormous sign with a

massive sparkly heart painted on it, overlying the words *Welcome Home.*

Home. Amen.

I run into his waiting arms, and the moment I'm close to him, I can breathe again. He wraps his arms around my waist and lifts me into the air, twirling me like we're some couple in a commercial for happy vacations. I guess we are that couple. The last year hasn't always been easy, but it's also been the most fun and the happiest of my life.

Luke gives the best hugs, the kind that make you feel entirely connected and wholly grounded. "I missed you, sunshine."

Instead of responding, I kiss him the way I've been dreaming about since he had to leave my tour in Paris. Mmm. Even after months apart, he still tastes like sweet creamy coffee with a hint of peppermint. He must have been experimenting at the cafe.

Luke cups my face in his hands, not releasing the connection between us, slipping his tongue between my lips.

"Come on." Luke takes my hand with his left and picks up my bag with his right. "Let's get you home."

I'm home at last.

"It's NOT fair that you look this good," I say.

He really does. The time in the tropical sunshine of Airlie Beach has made him glow with health. Or maybe it's the copious amount of phone sex we've had. I hold my hat down to keep it on my head as the breeze shifts through the buggy. "How's the cafe?"

"It's going great." He rests one hand on my thigh, and the pressure of his touch after so long without it practically has me panting. "Mom is thrilled to see you. I can't promise she didn't bake you seven dozen brownie cookies."

"Aww. Your mom is the best." I snuggle against his arm as we approach Airlie.

Luke kisses my cheek when we pause at a stop sign. "Any word from your parents?"

"Ugh." I roll my eyes. "I set them up with accounts out of the goodness of my heart, and they still can't help themselves. They have to ask for more repeatedly." I hesitate, but Luke senses it and squeezes my thigh. "My mom has been better. She says she wants to come out here sometime soon, if that's okay with you. I guess your mom reached out to her, and...I don't know." I play with the hem of my skirt. I picked this outfit just for him, a white A-line sundress with a pattern of tiny suns. Now it seems more like a convenient way to avoid complicated feelings. "Can't we go back to talking about how we missed each other?"

The curve of Luke's mouth is all wicked sin, and banishes every other thought from my mind. "Sunshine, I can't wait to show you exactly how much I've you."

I'M ON ALL FOURS, naked on the bed—no, *our* bed, which only makes me squee more—and I don't remember ever being this wet. Part of it is this view. The first time we saw this three-story house, the top two levels with full floor-to-ceiling windows overlooking the ocean, the view sold me. Who wouldn't want to wake up every morning with a view like this?

Unless, of course, you could wake up to Luke's head between your thighs, his perfect mouth clamped on your clit, but that's for me and me alone.

He smacks my ass playfully and I yelp, the brief hit of pain fading to red hot pleasure. "Are you ready, Nora?"

"Yes." I've been waiting for this. "I trust you."

He leans over me, the muscles of his body curling around

my front, and kisses me. "All right. Just relax. I'll stop any time you want."

I doubt I'll want him to stop. My default with Luke has been "yes." Should we move to the Whitsundays? Yes. Should we open a beachfront cafe with his mom as manager? Yes. Should I let him give me the best massage of my life then let him fuck me however he wants?

Absolutely.

He turns on soft instrumental music and I lie down on my front. There's a diffuser, too, spilling cascades of sweet spicy scent into the room. The only time I can relax is when I'm with him.

"Toys?" Luke asks, holding up a long feather.

"Definitely."

The feather glides across the skin of my back, tickling me. Luke runs it from my shoulders to my bottom, sweeping strokes and prickling sensation everywhere the feather lands. It's an odd sensation, being this turned on and simultaneously relaxed. When he runs the feather along the seam of my sex, the toy tickles me in a way that makes me giggle and laugh simultaneously.

Luke swallows it with a kiss. "More, sunshine?"

"More." More of this day. More of him. I can never tire of Luke. No one else makes me feel more connected in this world.

He switches from the feather to his hands, caressing the muscles of my back, my butt, my thighs. My arousal soaks the bed beneath us, and Luke takes pity on me, massaging my clit.

"I love you, Luke," I groan, pressing harder into his hand, seeking release.

"Love you, too, Nora."

He takes three fingers and slides them deep into my

vagina, and the feel of his hand inside me, stretching me, stroking my G spot, is unimaginable.

"Fuck, Luke, yes." I press against him, into his mouth, around his fingers, craving more. More. "You are the most perfect man."

"Good." He removes his hand from my canal, leaving me empty and wanting. "Do you want more, Nora?"

"Yes."

"Tell me what you want."

"Everything. Everywhere. You. I'm yours." I don't even know what I'm saying, but I feel empty, and I don't like it. "Please. Fill me up. Please."

He pauses, squeezing some lube from our omnipresent bottle into his hand. I press back against him, wanting him inside me again. "Can I touch you here, Nora?" He runs a finger down between my cheeks.

"Yes." I don't even hesitate. "Do it. Anything. I need to be filled."

"Whatever you want, sunshine." In one motion, he both slides his hot, hard cock into me and presses a knuckle into my ass. The combination is explosive. I cry out at the new sensation of his finger in me along with his cock, but the newness quickly changes to the most intense pressure. "Relax, Nora. Do you want me to stop?"

"No." I exhale, forcing myself to open, to take him deeper. Oh, yes. Now he hits exactly where I want him. I appreciate the feeling of him, everywhere.. Up until now, I've needed his hand on my clit to come, but like this? On my hands and knees, spread for him? "Luke, I love you so much. But I want you to go harder."

"I love you, too." He obeys, slamming his cock into me again and again until yes, that's it, I'm spiraling and clenching and crying out his name, always his name. There will never be anyone else for me. Luke. Always Luke.

He keeps thrusting through my climax until he joins me, his body contracting.

I never want anything but this. I never want anything but Luke. I travel the world and all I can think about is coming home to him.

Always.

IF YOU LIKE steamy vacation romances with a kink-focused travel agency, make sure to buy the other books in the International Desires series.

Want to know how Luke proposes in the Whitsundays? Get a bonus epilogue here for free by signing up for my mailing list!

ABOUT THE AUTHOR

NC Ross is the spicy sweet pen name of Natalie Cross. She writes stories with diverse characters, enthusiastic consent, high steam, and a little humor.

She currently lives in Los Angeles with a sweet rescue pup who may resemble a chicken nugget (as per her eight-year-old), and her family.